Red, the Wolf, and the Woods

Scarlett Gale

Published by Unnatural Redhead Creations, 2023.

This is a work of fiction. Similarities to real people, places, or events are entirely coincidental.

RED, THE WOLF, AND THE WOODS

First edition. September 1, 2023.

Copyright © 2023 Scarlett Gale.

ISBN: 979-8223906292

Written by Scarlett Gale.

This one's for the furries.

Red, the Wolf, and the Woods

ONCE UPON A TIME THERE was a little girl—

(Well, she was a little girl at one point, as many people are, but time marched on, so by the time our story reached her she had become a fully grown woman. She didn't know she was part of a story, which is usually how it went when you were in a story, unless the author was trying to do something very clever indeed.)

—who everyone called Little Red Riding Hood—

(This was her mother's nickname for her back when she was still a little girl. The only people who used it at the time this story takes place were said mother and the girl's brothers when they wanted to annoy her affectionately in the way of family. They always said it in a very cutesy voice. Seriously, you get really into wearing a red hooded riding coat for *one* winter and no one ever lets it go.

Anyway, for the purposes of our story, her name is Red.)

—and she was a brave and dutiful girl indeed—

(This is a euphemistic way of saying that, for all her parents' best efforts and personal belief in gender equality, Red's brothers frequently managed to wiggle their way out of chores in a way Red was never allowed to, so she had carried the majority of the work on their little farm since she was twelve years old. It was fine. She had made her peace with it, and with her brothers, who had gotten better about it once they were not asshole teenagers. The fact that she also stood to inherit the farm when her parents finally retired went a way toward soothing any hard feelings that might want to stick around, though at four in the morning in the dead of winter while she dragged on her muck boots, she often thought longingly of a much smaller property to manage. Maybe something further away from her brothers.)

—known throughout the village for being kind and patient with everyone, human and animal alike—

(Work as a farmer long enough, and you become an amateur vet, because *someone's* gotta take care of the livestock. Work with animals long enough as an amateur vet, and you learn what makes them tick. Work with *badly behaved* animals long enough, and you learn how to convince them to be less badly behaved in order to make both of your lives easier. Red wasn't just a dutiful, hardworking farmer's daughter—she had a lucrative side business running dog training lessons, and she was *this close* to having her cat and chicken circus ready to debut at the county fair. They don't usually lead with *that* in the stories.)

—and everyone loved her.

(She was reasonably well-liked—in spite of her incredibly busy schedule making it a challenge for her to properly socialize with her peers—unless you had an asshole dog you refused to train. Then she was probably your nemesis, but if you didn't want a nemesis, you should have trained your fucking dog.)

One morning, after Red finished her regular morning chores (farming meant morning chores, midday chores, afternoon chores, and evening chores (incidentally, we're done with the extended parenthetical asides now and back to normal parenthetical asides, probably)) she took advantage of the only spare fifteen minutes she was likely to have that day to relax with a massive cup of the truly horrible coffee her mother always brewed and a truly excellent chipotle cheddar scone her mother had baked. What her mother lacked in coffee brewing skills she made up for in baking, and Red rocked lazily in the front porch swing, enjoying her scone and tolerating her coffee. If she was lucky no one would come ask her for anything until she was done eating.

"Hey, no," she said collectively to Sparkles the chow mutt, Patches the terrier, Tater Tot the lab mix, and Frankenstein the chihuahua (probably) as they gathered around her muck-booted feet, seven and a half eyes (Frankenstein was named that for a reason) fixed hopefully on her scone and four tails wagging. "This has onion and garlic in it. Do you little freaks *want* liver failure?"

Sparkles indicated her deep desire for liver failure by putting one paw on the porch swing and whining. Frankenstein barked so hard he bounced in place, and then shut up at a quelling look from Red. Patches offered up his most pathetic facial expression, and Tater Tot just seemed happy to be involved. ("You look into that dog's eyes, and all you see is the back of her head," Red's mother once pronounced, and damn if she wasn't right.)

Red sighed and—accepting that she would never get a single moment to enjoy a snack on her own as long as she lived on this farm—wrapped her scone in a paper towel before tucking it into the front of her hoodie, where neither of the cats that had oozed onto the porch swing could get it. Camelia and Dirtbag were also very determined to give themselves liver failure.

(Yes, the hoodie was red. Shut up.)

"Okay, assholes," she said in a friendly tone, because dogs don't know they're being insulted if you insult them cheerfully, and sometimes they deserve to be insulted. (Like when they were interrupting her *only* breaktime.) "Everyone sit."

Three butts hit the porch. Red gave Tater Tot a *look,* and the fourth butt hit the porch slightly behind everyone else. Red gave it a minute—long enough for Patches to start wiggling in place—and when she judged everyone properly obedient, she tossed four treats in an arc like sowing seeds by hand.

Three mouths snapped said treats out of the air.

Tater Tot's treat hit the porch, her mouth snapping on nothing, and she looked affronted for a moment before snarfing it down.

"There you go," Red said, retrieving her scone. "Everyone lie down, now."

The dogs did—eventually—and that's where Red's mom found her five minutes later, scone devoured, coffee mug empty, and two cats squeezed onto her lap.

"Your grandma's out of hot sauce," Red's mom said with no preamble. "Can you run some out to her?"

"Who's gonna mulch if I do?" Red asked immediately, relieved that her mom hadn't appeared with a new, unexpected farm chore, and determined to use this as an excuse to wiggle out of an old, expected farm chore. Time to *herself*? Maybe she could manage to eat an entire *meal* without being harassed by dogs, or livestock, or brothers.

Red's mom considered the question and stuck her head back into the house. "Jason!" she yelled. "You're mulching today!"

"I was gonna go to Billy's!" Jason yelled back from upstairs, probably.

"Billy can come here and help you mulch!" Red's mom responded at volume.

"What about Red?" Jason shot back.

"Fuck off!" Red yelled cheerfully, too happy at the prospect of a walk in the woods to seem anything but. "Do I need to bring out the spreadsheet again?"

"Fine!" Jason managed to make it sound like he was grumbling even while he was yelling, which was pretty impressive. "I'll call Billy."

"Thank you!" Red's mom yelled, and turned to her. "Jason's going to do it."

"Thanks for the update," Red said dryly, attempting to extricate herself from the cats. "You sending her some scones, too?"

"I don't want to get disowned," Red's mom said, just as dryly, and strode back into the house.

Red's grandma lived in the deep woods, far away from the village, along a winding path through the forest that one shouldn't stray from, lest they be lost to its dangers forever.

That's what her parents told Red when she was a kid, anyway, because everything in a forest is dangerous when you're six. Red was twenty-six now, and the forest was as much her family as her grandma was. There were *chanterelles* in there! You could try to keep her out of it, but you'd fail, and probably trip on a fern in the process. (That was what her brothers found out the few times they tried to chase her in there, which was one of the many reasons she loved this forest.)

Now, because this wasn't the year 1367, Red's grandma's house was accessible by car. (How the fuck would they have built her house otherwise?) But the car route was a lot longer and took you way out of the village before doubling back through the forest, so unless Red *had* to bring a car, she usually rode her dirtbike out to the base of the winding path and walked up, which was what she did today. If she was offered the opportunity to visit her woods and dodge her chores in the process, she was going to take it, okay?

A weight fell away from her shoulders as she started up the path, like the stresses of the farm couldn't follow her once she was within the shade of the trees. The woods were wonderfully familiar, appearing still and calm if you were a city rube who couldn't recognize all the signs of an active, thriving forest ecosystem. Fortunately for Red, she was not a city rube, and she was able to identify multiple bird calls, say hello to several chipmunks, and pick some ripe salmonberries from a bush on the edge of the path. No one tried to steal the berries or asked her to do something they were capable of doing themselves, and the air smelled like fresh pine mulch instead of livestock. Perfect walk shit, if you asked her.

Of course, no sooner than she'd mentally described it as "perfect walk shit," something happened to make it significantly less perfect.

Red thought initially, when the form appeared through the trees, that someone's asshole dog had gotten loose. Then it got closer and she thought, *That's a big dog,* and then it stepped out into the dappled shade of the path and, okay, *holy shit—*

"What brings you out to these woods?" asked the Wolf, which was absolutely not a dog, but a fucking *wolf.* The fact that it—he?—could talk was honestly less surprising than the sudden appearance of a wolf in an ecosystem that had, up until now, only supported coyotes and the odd mountain lion on a wander through its extended territory.

Nature is healing, Red thought a little hysterically, but she'd been raised to be polite (by her parents) and to respect the natural magic of the world (by her grandma), and the Wolf (!!!) had asked her a question, so she took a deep, hopefully calming breath and said, "Just out on a walk." She took another breath that was less calming than she wanted it to be and added, "Nice day for it."

"It is indeed," the Wolf said, padding closer with his massive paws near silent on the path, ears pricked forward and his eyes unnervingly fixed on her. "May I join you?"

AAAAAAAAH! Red said, inside her head.

"I don't see why not," Red said out loud. *She* certainly wasn't about to tell a wolf she'd just met what he could and couldn't do. He probably shouldn't be this habituated to humans, right? Did normal rules about interacting with wolves apply when the wolf could talk? Like, Red's grandma was a witch, so it wasn't like Red had *zero* experience with the less conventional side of the world, but with all the time Red had to spend running the farm she wasn't able to dedicate much energy to witchcraft. Her grandma, wisely, focused on big stuff—treble bindings, avoiding mushroom circles, always being polite to anyone or anything that seemed out of the ordinary—and somehow the subject of talking wolves had never come up. Maybe Red's grandma assumed that they didn't have to worry about it, given the lack of wolves in the region. That seemed like a huge oversight now.

Belatedly, Red realized that she'd been standing awkwardly for far too long, and she forced her legs into movement. The Wolf stalked along next to her, seemingly docile, but every nerve in Red's body screamed about the presence of a large predator. The Wolf was... very big. And very wild-looking, with scruffy, ungroomed fur sticking up every which way. Were those brambles stuck behind his ear? What happened in her life to leave her walking close enough to a wolf to be able to tell if he had brambles stuck behind his ear?

Well. "You take life as it comes or die trying," Red's grandma always said. Granted, she hadn't been referencing talking wolves (presumably), but the advice still applied.

"I don't think I've seen you around before," she told the Wolf after an excruciating few minutes of silent walking, operating on the assumption that an awkward conversation would be less terrible than an awkward silence.

"I could say the same thing to you," the Wolf said in his deep, rumbling voice, giving her a sidelong look. Wow, those eyes were really yellow.

Red snorted, trying to ignore the weird jolt that came with the eye contact. "Sure, but I come out here once a week, so I think I win on familiarity grounds." Shit, are you not supposed to sass a talking wolf? Was sassing the kind of thing that would get you cursed?

The Wolf rumbled in a way that *seemed* thoughtful, but mostly just sounded like a growl. "I suppose that is fair." He had a strangely formal way of speaking, like he learned it from a grammar textbook. Maybe he did. Red didn't know how wolves learned to talk; there might as well be grammar textbooks involved. "I found myself here recently after a lot of traveling," he added after a moment.

Huh. Traveling. Red eyed the Wolf over again. Traveling would probably explain the messy fur and the brambles. Now that part of her brain had stopped screaming quite so loudly, she could actually note other things about the Wolf, like that his massive paws appeared extra massive because the rest of him was so rangy and thin. When he spoke she could see his gums, and they were pale enough to suggest an iron deficiency. The Wolf hadn't just been traveling—he must have been *starving*. Red felt a great, unwise pang of sympathy for him, and then remembered that she herself was made of delicious human meat and decided to remain wary of him instead.

"Do you plan to stay?" Red wanted to know the answer for multiple reasons, like whether or not she'd need to find a different route to her grandma's house, and specifically whether he would try to eat her if she kept using this one.

The Wolf cocked his head. "It would be nice to have a home," he said slowly, with maybe a hint of wistfulness. That was probably a yes, then.

"Don't rustle the sheep," Red advised, unable to stop herself from trying to help. "Or the goats. Or any of the livestock, not if you don't want to get shot."

The Wolf blinked at her once. "I shall take that under consideration." He licked his chops, which Red chose to interpret as being directed at the idea of eating a sheep, not because he was staring at her unblinkingly like he was separating her out into edible parts.

"*Seriously,*" Red stressed. "Stick to the woods. Eat deer. There are teenage boys who'll still probably try to hunt you if you're in here, but raiding the farms will be a death sentence." She wasn't sure why she felt obligated to help the Wolf stay safe, especially when he kept looking at her like she was a walking butcher's shop, but she knew she didn't want to see his corpse hanging halfway out of someone's battered old farm truck.

The Wolf blinked at her twice this time, perhaps surprised by her vehemence. "It is not a chore to stay in the forest," he said, ears flicking. "I find it pleasing out here."

"They're nice woods," Red agreed, pleased to have a topic of mutual conversational interest. She could talk about these woods literally all day. Even with wolves, apparently.

"They are," the Wolf replied, sounding amused. "They have seemed a bit lonely thus far, though, so I find the company is much improved today." He drifted closer to her on the path. Red automatically stepped away to keep herself out of biting range, and he meandered back to his original distance like the too-close interlude hadn't happened.

"Thanks," Red said after she was sure he was staying *over there*. Was this wolf trying to hit on her? Was that a thing wolves *did*? Like, in the old cartoons, sure, but in the real world?

The Wolf let that float in the air for a few more steps before asking, "What brings you out to these lovely woods so frequently, Miss...?"

"You can call me Red." Should she ask for the Wolf's name? Did wolves even have names? Would she be able to pronounce it if he did? "I like hiking," she added with deliberate vagueness, already annoyed at spilling the beans about the frequency of her visits. If this wolf *was* hitting on her (what the fuck) she wasn't about to give him more information about where to track her down. She knew how creeps creeped. (Also, she still wasn't sure he wasn't going to try to eat her, and she didn't want to make it easier for him to do *that*, either.) "There's a lot of great foraging out here."

The Wolf hummed in agreement, like the rumble of a distant garbage truck. "So it has nothing to do with the Witch who lives at the end of the path, or the cheese and flour I can smell in your backpack?"

Fuck. *Fuck.* This smug motherfucker. Red was still struggling for a response through the indignation when he sprang in front of her on the path, turning to block her way with his yellow eyes and his lethal teeth. "Terribly rude of you to lie to a new friend," he said in half a growl, head down and attention focused as he took a stalking step toward her. "Perhaps you should share your food with me to make amends."

That didn't require any thought at all to respond to, even through the terror.

"*No!*" Red snapped automatically, stomping a foot as she pointed at the Wolf accusingly. "That is *people* food! It is not for you! Do you want *liver failure?!*" Someone fucking save her from canines determined to poison themselves! (Maybe save her from getting eaten by a wolf, too!)

Before today Red wouldn't have thought wolves could look taken aback, but then, before today there were a lot of things she hadn't known about wolves. The Wolf looked at her pointing finger, then up to her face, and then eventually away, shuffling in place a bit. Some of the feral danger faded, replaced with melancholy.

"I suppose," he said with a definite level of sulk, "that I would prefer to avoid liver failure, yes."

"Good." Red realized she was still pointing and retracted her finger, bewildered at her own daring. She skirted around the Wolf as widely as she could and started walking again, because these scones (and the multiple bottles of homemade hot sauce) weren't going to deliver themselves, and also maybe if she walked far enough, she'd leave this weird dream world where yelling at talking wolves was a normal occurrence.

"A *true* friend would share their food with a hungry, lonely companion, though," the Wolf said another dozen yards or so down the path, casting her a pathetic look, all drooping ears and wide eyes. (It was somewhat spoiled by the way he licked his chops again, exposing an unholy level of fang.) "You have something else, do you not?"

Red considered this for a few steps. Feeding wildlife was a terrible idea for many reasons, but when a *talking wolf* walked up to you and asked for a snack in *human language* she didn't think that really counted as wildlife anymore. (Also, he was clearly underweight. If Red saw a dog in this condition she'd straight-up steal it from its owners to nurse it back to health without a single pang of conscience. Maybe if she made herself the *bearer* of food he wouldn't think of her *as* food.)

Eh, she thought to herself, *why not?* and drifted to a stop in the middle of the path, surrounded by ferns and shaded by sweet-smelling fir trees.

"Sit," she ordered automatically, reaching into her hoodie pocket for a dog treat.

The Wolf looked even *more* taken aback by this than by the pointing earlier. "I beg your pardon?"

Okay, yeah, that was... weird. Ordering around someone that could talk was *very* weird, objectively, but Red couldn't back down now. If she did, he'd only ever see her as a subordinate, which—since her goal for the day was to not get eaten—would be extremely counterproductive. She held up the dog treat and raised an eyebrow expectantly. "*Sit.*"

The Wolf glared at her.

Red raised the other eyebrow.

The Wolf glared harder.

Red remained implacable. She'd trained dogs that *couldn't* talk. This was nothing.

The Wolf snarled at her wordlessly. (Yep, still a terrifying level of fang!)

Red did nothing, though her heart rate kicked into what she hoped was its highest gear, because if it went any faster she might pass out, and the Wolf would have free rein to eat her.

The Wolf's eyes flicked from her face to the hand with the dog treat. He licked his chops. (Red really wished he'd stop flashing those teeth.) He switched back to looking at her face again.

He sat down, looking deeply angry about it.

"Good boy," Red praised—apparently she was incapable of feeding an animal a treat without doing this—and tossed it to him. The Wolf snapped it out of the air (TEETH!) and ate it with a strange expression. (You know, compared to the other expressions she'd seen on *the talking wolf* so far.)

"Thank you," he said almost politely, standing with a big stretch and then stalking toward her pocket. "Are there more?"

"If you're good," Red said, giving herself over to the weirdness of the whole situation but *definitely* still keeping herself out of biting range. She pulled out another treat. "Wanna catch?"

Yes. The answer was definitely yes. They walked, and Red tossed dog treats into the woods at random whenever she felt like it, and each time the Wolf snarfed it out of the air almost too quickly to see. He got *air,* too! He could probably jump straight over her head if he tried, but that seemed a little too much like tempting a mauling. (She was using this as a technique to keep him as far away from her as possible, anyway.) It was both unnerving and fun, being the center of a cyclone of wolf violence, and when Red reached into her pocket to find nothing but lint, it was too soon.

"I'm out," she said, spreading her empty hands. "Sorry."

The Wolf growled wordlessly, trotting in loops around her. "But I am still *hungry.*"

Red shrugged, pretending to be casual while guilt and fear twisted in her belly. "You'll have to go hunting," she said bluntly. "Seriously, these scones are full of poison for you. I don't have anything else I can share."

The Wolf grumbled something she couldn't quite make out and prowled around her in a long, slow, considering circle, his attention focused and deadly. It prickled the hair on the nape of her neck, her fight-or-flight reflex rising back up and settling on *fight.* Red hadn't *forgotten* that the Wolf was a wolf, but the cold, predatory light in his eyes legitimately made her feel like she might pee her pants.

"Very well," the Wolf said eventually, flopping over onto his side with a theatrical sigh in such a parody of disappointment that it almost convinced Red that there had never been any danger. (Would a wolf know what sighing theatrically meant? Did wolf theater exist? If so, how could Red watch it?) "I suppose this is where I shall take my leave, then."

Red smashed down her lingering panic and the weird disappointment (she had a lot of questions about talking wolves) and the guilt that she couldn't offer more. "It was nice to meet you," she said, also smashing down the urge to ruffle his ears. (That was not a thing you should do to wolves!)

"You as well," the Wolf said, climbing back to his feet and—oh wow! Yikes!—darting in to rub his shoulder against her legs like a friendly dog before she could dodge. (He could move *fast,* apparently!) He looked up at her with those big, yellow eyes, and grinned with all his teeth. "I hope we meet again soon, Miss Red."

And then he was gone into the woods, and she was as alone as she'd ever been.

"Yeah," Red said a bit distantly, trying to get her heart rate to come down from that last spike of adrenaline. "Yeah, me too."

Red had nearly convinced herself that she hallucinated the entire interlude with the Wolf by the time she made it to her grandma's house some fifteen minutes later. Her little brother Teddy almost got taken by a will-o-the-wisp when they were younger, so it wasn't like the forest deciding to prank her with a talking wolf was completely out of the realm of possibility.

The decided lack of her dog treats and the gray fur stuck to the leg of her jeans were a pretty strong indicator of the actual existence of the talking wolf, though, so...

"Grandma?" she asked, pushing open the front door of the cottage and noting as she did that it was unlatched. "I brought you some hot sauce. And scones."

No answer. That wasn't too weird. Red's grandma spent a lot of time out in her gardens or foraging in the forest. (Red had to learn it somewhere, and in their limited time together, her grandma was determined to teach her as much as they both could manage.) Red headed for the kitchen to unload, because she was used to carrying heavy stuff around, but a backpack full of hot sauce really did a number on the shoulders.

"Grandma?" she called again, lining up the bottles neatly. "You here?"

"In here," responded a wavering voice from the direction of the bedroom, one that absolutely did not sound like Red's grandma and instead sounded like someone with a very deep voice attempting a falsetto. "I seem to have fallen ill, dear child." The voice followed this up with two very fake coughs.

Yeah, that was definitely not Red's grandma, from whose magical cleaning concoctions infectious diseases ran screaming in fear and who only ever referred to Red as "Kiddo." All the hair on Red's body stood up, a fresh surge of adrenaline leaving her both calm and furious at the same time. Who the fuck broke into her grandma's house? Where was her grandma?

"That's terrible," she said evenly, scanning the living room for signs of a struggle and finding none. Good. Her grandma was probably outside, then. "Do you want me to bring you some tea?"

Two more incredibly fake coughs. "Just some water would be lovely, dear child."

Being called "dear child" was possibly the grossest experience of Red's life, and that included all the sheep afterbirth. She made a face and went for the sink, filling the largest, heaviest mug in the kitchen. (It was one Jason made when he was six. It said "Worldz gratest Grama" and weighed approximately five pounds when empty.) Should she get a knife? Was she willing to stab whoever was in her grandma's bedroom? Surely the mug would be a workable improvised weapon. If she brought a knife, then there was a possibility of losing the knife, and Red would rather bet on defending herself from a big mug than from a knife. Decision made.

Red took a few deep breaths before she headed for the main bedroom, aware that this was the worst possible decision to be making. If she was sensible she'd leave, find her grandma, and then come back with a shotgun or a cursed walnut she could throw. (Why hadn't she taken her grandma up on that offer to learn hexes? Why hadn't she *made* herself take time away from the farm so she *could* take her grandma up on that offer to learn hexes?!) She'd always considered herself sensible, before, but now she might have to give up on that self-descriptor. This was a horror movie mistake she found herself in the middle of making, but people shouldn't be breaking into her grandma's house! If people thought they could get away with breaking into her grandma's house and then calling her "dear child" like a fucking creep, it was absolutely her job to disabuse them of that notion with a *vengeance*.

"How are you feeling, Grandma?" Red called as she walked down the hall with steady, measured steps, hands barely shaking where they clenched around the mug.

"Very weak and tired, dear child," definitely-not-Red's-grandma answered, with another couple extremely fake coughs. "Are you bringing me water?" *Why* was that voice weirdly familiar?

"Of course, Grandma." Okay. There was the door to the bedroom. Red just had to open it up and see what the fuck was happening here. If only she could get her hands to work.

"Dear child?" the voice asked, high and wavering. "Are you there? Do you have the water?" More of that awful coughing. Had this person never heard a *cough* before? "Bring me the water, dear child."

Who does this motherfucker think they are, ordering me around? Red thought fiercely, forcing her fear into anger through willpower alone. *They break into my grandma's house and impersonate her and then try to assign me chores? Fuck that.* What an asshole. Unacceptable! They were going to regret all their life choices by the time she was done with them.

Red opened the door.

This was less dramatic than perhaps hoped, as all it revealed was her grandma's bedroom with the blinds shut and the lights off. It did nothing to defuse the tension, anyway.

"Grandma?" she asked, not that she was expecting any kind of *real* answer, but surely if whoever-the-fuck thought she was fooled, that would help her get the drop on them.

"Come closer, dear child," said the voice, which was even more obviously not her grandma's voice with the barrier of the door gone. "I'm so terribly tired." A strange, lingering pause, and then it whispered, "And *hungry*."

Oh! Good! Super creepy! Nothing ominous about that at all. Red swallowed and forced herself to take a step into the room, ready for anything but not at all sure what she should be ready for—

The light from the hall cast itself across the bed as she moved, revealing a lump under the covers, a dark shape against the pillows, and a yellow, gleaming, *familiar* eye.

"What the fuck do you think you're doing under the covers?" Red's mouth asked without waiting for input from the rest of her.

"The better to—what?" said the Wolf, getting off track there in the middle and dropping into his normal deep rumble. "I mean." The horrible grandma impression came back. "Resting, dear child."

Red snorted. "Yeah, while you're creeping on me with those big ol' fucking wolf peepers? Who do you think you're fooling?"

"I'm old and unwell," the Wolf insisted, like her eyes hadn't adjusted and she couldn't see his whole wolf head, ears and fur and fangs and all. "Bring me my water, dear child."

"Okay," Red said with a shrug.

She threw the water right in his face. The water from her grandma's well was ice-cold, even in the height of summer, which made it very refreshing when you wanted a drink and nearly painful when you needed to rinse your teeth after brushing. The Wolf apparently found it shockingly cold, because he yelped and scrambled to his feet, shaking out his fur with no regard for the fact that he was shedding water all over Red's grandma's sheets.

"You *impertinent*—" he snarled, then yelped again when the extremely heavy mug thumped hard into his shoulder.

"Get out!" Red snapped, pointing at the door. "Off the bed! Out! *Out!*"

The Wolf snarled wordlessly, a flash of white teeth in the dark, and leapt at her, which, yes, was somewhat terrifying, but he wasn't actually bigger than the Collins's ill-bred Great Dane, and Red had that dog wrapped around her pinkie.

"Down!" she ordered, kneeing the Wolf in the chest so hard he flew into the corner of the mattress with a thump. "No jumping!"

"I will rend you limb from limb," the Wolf growled, scrambling back to his feet. He lunged again, jaws wide, and when his teeth closed around Red's arm pure, terrified, bone-deep instinct took over her body. She set her feet and *shoved,* driving him back and driving her arm into the back of his throat at the same time. Red shoved harder than she meant to, actually, knocking him into the side of the bed and leaving him gagging around her forearm.

"*No! Biting!*" she yelled in his face as he scrabbled at her wildly, shaking his head and trying to escape her pin. He managed to get a hind leg up against her stomach, enough power behind it to kick her away. The Wolf shook his head, flexing his jaw in obvious discomfort. (He was lucky she hadn't dislocated it, frankly.)

Red rebounded off the wall he'd kicked her into and struck in his moment of distraction, scruffing the Wolf with both hands and hauling him bodily out of the bedroom. He struggled, and she yanked him up by said scruff until his forepaws barely brushed the ground and hauled faster.

"What are you—" he tried, claws dragging against the wood floor in a way not unlike nails on a chalkboard.

"You can fuck right off," Red told him. She managed to kick the front door open (thank fuck for her grandma's latch handles) and yanked the Wolf outside.

"Red?" her grandma asked from the corner of the house in tones of great alarm.

"I will flay the flesh from your bones!" yowled the Wolf.

"I'm handling it!" yelled Red, marching toward the woods with a snarling, whining bundle of angry wolf limbs doing its level best to impede her progress. The adrenaline carried her all the way into the underbrush, thorns catching at her jeans, and she *launched* the fucking Wolf into the bushes like a shotput. (Or something. Red wasn't sure what throwing a shotput was like. She never did track and field.) The Wolf crashed at least ten feet into the treeline before he recovered enough to catch his balance, and he whipped around with his head down and his eyes flaring.

"You *little*—" he snapped, leaping at her with murder in his eyes. Red caught him with a muck boot and two hundred and twenty-four pounds of angry farmer behind it, kicking him in the chest and sending him yelping into the woods again.

"Get the *fuck* out!" she bellowed. "You are *not* welcome here! *Bad wolf!*"

The Wolf snarled at her wordlessly, climbing to his feet with obvious difficulty, and he fled into the trees with his tail between his legs. Red watched him go, panting for breath, furious and still shaking and absolutely not worried at all about whether she broke any of his ribs with that last kick.

"Okay," Red's grandma said, setting a hand on her shoulder. "So." A comforting pat. "What the fuck was that?"

"Wolf," Red said between gasps. "Talking."

Red's grandma sucked her teeth for a moment. "Huh." She patted Red's shoulder again. "Well, come inside, kiddo, and tell me all about it when you're done with your panic attack."

"Sure thing, Grandma," Red said with a weak, trembling laugh, and with one last look at the woods, she followed her grandma into the cottage.

Normally the story would end here, with Little Red Riding Hood and her grandmother safe, and with the Wolf defeated.

Normally there would be a woodcutter.

Normally there would be blood.

Our story isn't over yet.

A week later found Red standing at the entrance to the path through the woods to her grandma's house. It was a week where Red kept an eye out and an ear to the ground and saw and heard neither hide nor hair of the Wolf. He might have left entirely, but if he was still in the woods, he was staying in the woods and not messing with the farms. Small favors, Red supposed.

(If he left, that would have been the best possible option. This was no place for a wolf. Red *wanted* the Wolf to be gone. She certainly hadn't spent the last week remembering the limp he'd had when he'd fled into the woods, or wondering if there was enough wild prey to let him gain the weight he needed and sustain him for the long-term. There definitely weren't any nights where she laid awake, staring at the ceiling with her mind churning with worry. Absolutely nothing like that had happened.)

Was it foolish of her to go into the forest now, knowing the Wolf might still be lurking? Maybe. But Red's grandma called down because she ran out of trash bags, and Red was happy enough to a) get a couple of uninterrupted, uninterruptible hours to herself and b) get out of chicken coop duty, and the fact remained that driving would take way longer and—crucially—not involve a walk in the woods. These were Red's woods. She *loved* these woods. They were her territory before the Wolf moved in, and like hell she was going to cede them to that rude motherfucker now.

The fact that Red dithered where she was for at least another full minute was neither here nor there, and if you asked her about it after the fact, she'd tell you she hadn't done it.

Red slipped a hand into her hoodie pocket, running her thumb over the canister inside. This was fine. She would be fine.

She stepped onto the path.

The path was empty. It smelled like fir needles and fresh air. It was dappled with sunlight through the trees. It looked as it usually did: Like a well-worn path through the woods.

It was all very anticlimactic.

Red sighed at herself and started walking.

The walk also went as it usually went, quiet and contemplative and very uphill. Red stayed on high alert as she climbed, eyes scanning the underbrush and the trees, ears metaphorically pricked for anything out of the ordinary. There was nothing but the sound of birds and the occasional small animal in the leaf litter.

I guess he's gone, Red thought, right as she came around a small bend in the path and found the Wolf sitting in the middle of it, because even when you don't know you're in a story, thinking that kind of thing is almost a guarantee to summon the thing you're thinking about.

Red froze from the hips-down. Her hand, primed to do this very thing, whipped the canister out of her pocket and held it at the ready. She sure as fuck wasn't relying on her *boots* this time.

(She was also wearing the study boots, obviously. She just wasn't *relying* on them.)

The Wolf made eye contact with her briefly, nostrils flaring. He blinked, shook himself, and—instead of snarling or charging her or any of the myriad things she was expecting—laid down on his belly.

"Miss Red," he said solemnly, the bass rumble of his voice carrying easily through the silence between them.

"I'm back to 'Miss' now?" Red asked, hands trembling minutely. "What happened to 'impertinent'?"

The Wolf winced and looked off into the woods. "I apologize for that."

Red didn't let the surprise show, even though it was *definitely* there. "And the part where you said you'd rip the flesh from my bones?"

The Wolf's ears twitched, and his eyes shut in an even more obvious wince. "It was 'flay,'" he said with what sounded like genuine regret, "and I apologize for that as well."

Red frowned. This wasn't where she was expecting this encounter to go. (Granted, she hadn't had expectations for this encounter, but if she'd had, this wouldn't have even made the list.)

The Wolf opened his eyes and looked at her head on, ears tucked back and his tail wrapped tightly around his back haunches. "I have hoped, since last week, to be able to properly apologize to you." His ears twitched again. "For all of it."

Red frowned harder. Definitely unexpected. She considered the distance between them, the Wolf's body language, and how quickly she could bring the canister to bear before allowing some of the primed readiness to drop from her posture.

"Fine," she said, trying to project impatience. "Carry on."

The Wolf pushed slowly back up to sitting, posture as straight as possible for a *fucking wolf.* He regarded her silently for a moment in utter stillness, eyes narrowed in thought instead of anger.

"My behavior when last we met was unconscionable," he said with careful enunciation. "I was... not well, I now realize, but that is no excuse for how I acted. I am deeply sorry for what I did, and I hope you can accept my sincere apology." The Wolf's eyes tracked down to her arm, and his ears drooped slightly. "Did I injure you?"

"Scratches," Red admitted, holding up her forearm and displaying the holes he managed to rip in her hoodie with his fangs. (Yes, she was still wearing it. It was a work hoodie to begin with. The holes were part of the point.)

The Wolf's ears drooped even more pathetically, and he whined low in his throat. "I apologize for that, as well."

"Thank you for apologizing," Red said automatically, because she was raised to be polite. She did not say, "That's fine," because she was also raised not to allow people to think an apology fixed everything they fucked up when shit was still fucked. "Was that all?" she asked after a moment, when the Wolf made no moves to say or do anything else.

The Wolf swallowed visibly, back to not quite making eye contact. "I understand if the answer is no," he started hesitantly, "but I very much enjoyed our conversation last week—"

"Funny way of showing it," Red muttered, not bothering to make it quiet.

The Wolf winced again and nodded, conceding the point. "I had hoped you might consider letting me walk with you until you reach the end of the path," he said, lying back down on the ground and generally trying to make himself as small and non-threatening as possible. "I would be grateful for the company."

"Why?" Red asked, both genuinely curious and wanting to push him a little. What was he up to?

His tail thumped the ground twice, and he looked away into the woods. "I have been alone for... a long time."

"Is that an excuse?" Red asked evenly.

The Wolf tilted his head, gazing up at her out of the corner of one golden eye. "No." He sighed. "It is... an explanation."

"Hmph," Red said, and let him stew in silence for probably a full minute without changing her facial expression in the slightest. It was a technique she frequently used on human men who'd just said something inappropriate, and frequently resulted in spontaneous apologies when deployed correctly. The Wolf looked progressively more and more uncomfortable as the seconds ticked by, but he didn't leave. He kept eye contact (with her left shoulder—he was a predator, she couldn't fault him for not wanting to keep *true* eye contact) and his tail thumped the ground a few more times, but he waited out her silence with an impressive level of patience.

"You're not going to try and eat me again?"

The Wolf frowned, flinching in a way that looked almost offended. Red pointed at him accusingly. "Hey, it's a fair question. You tried it once."

The Wolf frowned again, but more thoughtfully this time. "That," he said evenly, "is a reasonable point." He shook himself and sat up to face her head on. "No. I will not attempt to eat you again, today or ever."

Pretty good. Not good enough. "Swear it," Red ordered. "Swear it three times."

The Wolf gave her a look that seemed almost startled, as though it was a surprise that Red knew the old laws. "You would have me bound to you?"

Red shrugged. She'd rather have him bound and sworn to safety than wandering around free and dangerous. Was it a bad idea? Maybe. Did she have a better one? No.

The Wolf regarded her for another long moment and nodded. "I swear I mean you no harm," he started, deep voice rumbling with steady power. "I swear that as long as you walk in my presence, I will allow no harm to come to you. I swear I will respect you, and your grandmother the Witch, and the rules you make for me."

The woods around them went entirely silent for a moment, the Wolf's words echoing out into the trees as though to replace the missing sound. It was uncanny the way the trees sucked up the noise, like the way Red thought the vacuum of space would draw the air out of a damaged ship. She could hear her own heartbeat, and the Wolf's, and it was *horrible,* the thumping was so *loud,* what *was* this—

A bluejay screamed somewhere nearby, and the strange moment broke, sound rushing back in to fill the void like water into the depression caused by a flung rock. Red staggered slightly. The Wolf whined, shaking his head. For a breath longer, Red could hear both their hearts beating in time, and before she could even exhale the strangeness stopped. Was it ever there? Or was it a figment of her imagination?

The Wolf shook himself head to tail and sat again, golden eyes patient and ears attentive. "Is that sufficient?"

Red let him squirm for a bit longer, considering. "Yeah," she said finally, shoulders dropping a little. She raised her hand with the canister and waggled it at him. "But you should know I have pepper spray, and I am absolutely willing to hit you with it if you step out of line even a *little* bit."

The Wolf did something confused around the eyebrows. "I do not know what pepper spray is," he admitted.

"And you'll keep it that way if you know what's good for you," Red told him firmly. She hitched the straps of her backpack a bit more securely over her shoulders and jerked her chin at the trail. "Shall we?"

The Wolf trotted to the side of the trail (the side on which Red had the pepper spray, she noted with interest) and waited patiently for her to start walking before he fell in beside her. Red didn't let her attention waver and kept the pepper spray pointed in his direction. The treble-vow (what a fucking pretentious name for it) was an indicator of good intent, but Red's grandma had made sure she knew it wasn't foolproof. If the Wolf tried some shit, it wouldn't be good for him, but that wouldn't mean much if he managed to rip out her throat before the backlash hit.

The Wolf did not go for her throat. Instead, after about five minutes of silent walking, the Wolf cleared his throat almost awkwardly and ventured, "How have you been since last we met?"

"Since you tried to eat me?" Red asked. Just because he had apologized didn't mean she wasn't going to rub it in to make him feel bad at every opportunity.

The Wolf lashed his tail and whined low in his throat, almost inaudibly. "Yes," he said, eyeing her sidelong. "Since then."

Red considered the question. "Well enough." She couldn't remember a single thing she'd done in the past week, which was usually what happened when someone asked what she'd been up to. "The donkey got out again."

The Wolf made an interested noise. "Again?"

"She's a fucking asshole," Red said, exasperated even though the asshole donkey was nowhere nearby to exasperate her. "Too smart for her own good. She figured out how to unlatch her stall when she was little, and now she's a terror."

The Wolf made another interested, expectant noise, and Red told him all about Jackass the donkey, and how every time they thought they'd managed to find a way to keep her in her stall, Red would head to the barn a week later to find Jackass happily digging through the bagged grain, or browsing with the chickens, or standing directly outside the door to her stall with a cat asleep on her back and a look on her equine face like, "*What else did you expect?*"

"I think what I'm doing is accidentally training a donkey escape artist," she said with a sigh. "I'm going to have to go on tour with donkey Houdini."

"I do not know who that is," the Wolf said politely, "but I am sure you would draw a crowd."

They walked in silence for a few steps, the dappled sunlight playing over them, before Red asked, "What about you?"

The Wolf visibly startled. "Me?"

Red nodded. "How have you been since you tried to eat me?"

He considered that, trotting along at the edge of the trail, where the ferns and brambles curled into the path. "I have been better than I was when we met," he said eventually. "This forest has good hunting."

"Mmm-hmm," Red said pointedly. He *did* look better, though—his fur was shinier, with no brambles, and there was less of a haunted look around his eyes. Still too skinny, though.

"Good hunting for *game;* I brought down a deer," the Wolf clarified. After another pause he added, "I had not realized as much yet, last time. I had only just arrived." A considering breath. "There was much I did not know."

Red actively decided to let that sit rather than trying to address it. "I haven't seen you around the farms." It wasn't quite a question.

"Of course not," the Wolf said immediately. "You told me to stay away."

"And you always do what you're told?" Red asked, one eyebrow arched skeptically.

"I always take good advice when it is from reliable sources," the Wolf said, not quite looking at her. His steps slowed. "Ah. We have arrived."

Red glanced up and found to her surprise that he was right. Her grandma's house sat in its clearing at the end of the path, like it always did, only Red hadn't even *noticed* they'd gotten this close. Why hadn't she noticed? Was it really *that* distracting to talk to someone who seemed like they actually wanted to listen, and didn't talk over her like she didn't exist? She wouldn't know; she'd never had that happen before.

"Well, then, Miss Red," the Wolf said, turning to face her and sitting down neatly. "Thank you for letting me accompany you today."

He flicked his ears, something unknowable in those golden eyes. "I very much appreciate the conversation, and the second chance."

"Thank you for apologizing," Red said. "And for not trying to eat me again."

The Wolf blinked slowly. "I gave you my word," he said simply, as though that mattered to most people.

"You did," Red allowed, because she could tell it mattered to *him*. She slid her non-pepper-spray hand into her hoodie pocket and let him sit there for a moment longer while she thought. Should she? She really couldn't *not,* not with him sitting so obediently and his perfect behavior for the whole walk.

"Good boy," she said, withdrawing her hand and tossing him three dog treats at once. He snapped them out of the air in a flash of white teeth, offered her a slack-jawed canine grin, and disappeared into the forest.

Weird, Red decided as she watched him go. *Weird, but not bad.*

She wondered if she'd ever see him again.

She saw him again.

He met her at the foot of the path the next time Red's mom sent her up to grandma's, this time with a backpack full of fresh eggs and smoked salmon. (Her uncle had visited and brought with him the fruits of his fishing labor, to everyone's delight, especially Red's, since running to her grandma's meant she got to avoid mucking out the stable today.) She barely stepped foot into the woods before he appeared at the edge of the undergrowth, ears pricked forward and tail wagging gently.

"Miss Red," he said with what seemed like genuine enthusiasm. "It is a pleasure to see you. May I walk with you again today?"

"Are you that hard up for company?" Red asked, retrieving her pepper spray and not trying to hide it in the least.

The Wolf gave her a dry look. "Have you met any other talking animals in this forest? Because if you have, I would appreciate an introduction."

Red raised her eyebrows at him. "Are you sassing me now?"

The Wolf blinked slowly and said nothing. Definitely sass. He must have been feeling better, because he sure hadn't had a sense of humor before.

"Yeah, sure," Red decided out loud with a mental shrug. She was walking that way anyway, and she was pretty sure he wouldn't try to eat her again, and if he did try shit, she still had the pepper spray. "Come on, then."

The Wolf shook himself, ears flapping, and trotted along the edge of the path at a careful, polite distance. "How is your donkey? Still a menace?"

"She's teamed up with the dogs now," Red said with great exasperation. "It's a fucking nightmare. What about you?" She glanced at him. It probably was too early to tell if he'd put on any weight under the fluff, but his fur was significantly sleeker than she remembered it from last week, and he was moving less gingerly.

"I have been well," the Wolf said. He glanced over at her and they made eye contact before Red snapped her face back forward, feeling like she'd been caught staring. "The deer in these woods are exceptionally foolish," he added. "They have been comically easy prey."

"They won't stay that way for long," Red pointed out, ignoring the satisfied feeling in her belly of knowing the Wolf had been eating well.

"Then I am doing them a favor," the Wolf said with deep gravitas, and Red snorted a laugh. He preened a little in her peripheral vision, like making her laugh was an accomplishment or something, and Red efficiently crushed down any warm emotions that idea inspired. She might not know what his endgame was, but he was still a wolf. She wasn't going to let her guard down.

The walk to Red's grandma's place went faster with company once again, and Red was in the middle of a story involving two dogs, a cat, and a younger brother when it suddenly appeared in front of them. She trailed off a bit awkwardly. Already? Wait, no, this was the goal. She should be happy to be here.

"I shall take my leave, then," the Wolf said politely, drawing her out of her thoughts. "Thank you, again, for the company." He sat down, eyes on her expectantly. To look at him you'd never think that two-ish weeks previously he'd attempted to maul her.

"It was a nice walk," Red said honestly. She watched him with one hand in her hoodie pocket, wondering if he'd ever actually ask for what he wanted or if he'd just try to wait there until the heat death of the universe.

Approximately thirty seconds later Red decided that *she* didn't want to wait until the heat death of the universe, and she tossed him a handful of dog treats with a, "Good boy." The Wolf snapped three of them out of the air, snarfed the other two up off the ground, and darted into the woods with a bounce to his gait like her pocketful of dog treats was the best thing to happen to him all day.

Red watched him go, amused and a bit bewildered, and made a note to see if he liked the freeze-dried chicken liver treats the cats went wild for.

...Assuming she saw him again, of course.

The Wolf liked the chicken liver treats.

He also very much liked the dried beef chews, though Red decided that the better part of valor involved not telling him that they were made from steer penises.

(Not that she thought he'd care, really, but it seemed awkward to tell a sapient animal he was chewing on a dick, even if that sapient animal would happily eat any part of an entire steer, including the dick. Anyway. Red didn't tell him, was the point.)

The next time Red went to her grandma's, the Wolf met her at the base of the path (as expected) and then followed her into the clearing to her grandma's door (not expected). Red kept her pepper spray (always in the hand closest to the Wolf) readied as she knocked. He'd been nothing but polite since that first time, but...

"Hey, kiddo!" Red's grandma said as she opened the door, and then, "Oh, and hello to you as well, Wolf."

"Ms. Witch," the Wolf said, tail wagging. "I hope we find you well?"

"Can't complain," Red's grandma said with a laugh. "Oh, well, I could, but if I did, the universe would hear me and then curse me so I had twice as much to complain about, so I'd better not. Did you bring me my romances?" The last was directed at Red, and was the only part of the conversation that made any sense.

"You could just have them delivered here, you know," Red pointed out, jiggling the strap on her backpack pointedly.

"Tell that to the postal system," Red's grandma said with the exasperation of someone who lived at the end of a very long gravel driveway in a town easily fifty miles away from the nearest large postal sorting center, not that Red had heard that particular rant on multiple occasions or anything. "Also, this way I get to see my favorite granddaughter, and make my grandsons actually pull their weight while you're here."

"I'm her only granddaughter," Red said to the Wolf, for some reason she didn't understand.

"That does not preclude you from being her favorite granddaughter," the Wolf said with good humor.

"Got it in one," Red's grandma said, snapping her fingers and pointing approvingly at the Wolf. "You coming in?"

The Wolf shook his head. "I will leave the two of you to your afternoon," he said, shifting from paw to paw. "I have business elsewhere in the forest today."

He didn't leave, though. Red looked at him. She looked at her grandma. Her grandma looked back, clearly holding back a smile, and jerked her chin like, "*Get on with it.*"

"Good boy," Red said, tossing the Wolf an entire dried chicken breast jerky treat. As soon as his teeth closed around it he was off, gray fur gleaming in the sunlight like finely polished silver before he disappeared into the woods.

Red got thirty beautiful seconds of blissful silence before her grandma said, "*So,*" in tones of anticipatory glee.

"It's called *positive reinforcement,*" Red snapped, elbowing past her into the house.

"Sure it is," Red's granny said with a knowing smile. "Come on, I made pie."

The pie was not an entirely sufficient repayment for the interrogation Red's granny put her through, but it was a really good fucking pie, so... Fine.

"You putting out snares?" Red asked two weeks later, running her fingers over the spectacular plumage from a pheasant laid out on her grandma's coffee table. They were new feathers, she could tell. They practically still smelled like the forest.

"Hmm?" Red's grandma leaned out of the kitchen, eyebrows raised, and took in the scene. "Oh, no, that's not me." She came in with their mugs of tea and settled into her favorite rocking chair. "It's from our mutual friend."

"The Wolf?" As though it could possibly be anyone else. "He visits you?" As though Red didn't already know that, with the humiliating conversation her grandma inflicted upon her the last time she stopped by.

"And brings gifts when he does," Red's grandma said, eyes bright and sharp above the rim of her mug as she sipped. "Seems to be trying to get into my good graces."

"He *did* try to eat me," Red pointed out. "And broke into your house to do it."

Red's grandma nodded. "Difficult first meeting, to be sure." She took a sip in the way that meant she was about to unleash something devastating. "And yet you let him walk you here every time you come see me." She paused. "And you're coming to see me more regularly than you used to."

Red shrugged. Those were definitely things she wasn't allowing herself to interrogate, so she saw no reason to let her grandma interrogate them, either.

Red's grandma let the silence stretch for another minute and finally took a sip of her tea. "He's useful, anyway," she said cheerfully. "The chipmunks don't dare step foot in my garden with him around."

"They didn't dare step foot in your garden before," Red said with a raised eyebrow. "On account of the curses."

"But now I don't have to cast the curses, so he's saving me a lot of time and effort," her grandma parried smoothly. She glanced at the table and added, "Tasty bird, too."

"Well, as long as the bird's tasty," Red said dryly, and sipped her tea.

The Wolf appeared at the edge of the path almost as soon as Red's foot hit it next time, ears pricked forward and tail wagging. "Miss Red," he said, doing a formal little canine bow. "Would you please come with me?"

Red paused, hand already going for her pepper spray. "Why?"

"A surprise," the Wolf said, obviously excited. He caught her expression and added, "It is not a surprise that involves violence against you or any other living creature."

Red relaxed slightly. Only slightly, though. "Is there a reason for the specificity of the latter half of that sentence?"

The Wolf made a movement startlingly like a shrug. "Though I gather from your farm stories you are fairly accustomed to dealing with death, I assumed it would not please you to watch me hunt and kill a rabbit."

Red blinked, a little surprised. Yes, she had told him about the necessary end she sometimes brought to the farm chickens when they got too old, but she hadn't expected him to really listen, let alone remember. "You were correct," she said when her mouth was once again in working order. "How far is this little detour?"

"Not far," he promised. "We will have you to the Witch's house with plenty of time before it gets dark."

Given the early sunset this deep into autumn, Red assumed that meant maybe a fifteen minute walk. "Sure," she decided, hitching her backpack up on her shoulders. "But if this is a trick, I *will* pepper spray you."

"And I would deserve it," the Wolf said good-naturedly, turning and padding away into the underbrush. He paused to glance over his shoulder at her. "I believe I have worked out the route that will be most comfortable for you, but try to step where I step." His brows furrowed a bit. "The ground here is less stable than the forests where I came from."

"Yeah, it's entirely comprised of rotten holes full of fir needles," Red said, holding herself back from an eye roll by sheer force of will. "This was my forest before it was yours."

The Wolf blinked once in surprise before his golden eyes went chagrined. "Of course. My apologies."

Red was not used to being apologized to without a lot of prompting on her part, and she hadn't yet figured out how to feel about it. "We're losing light," she said instead of anything else. "Where's your surprise?"

The Wolf's jaw dropped open, a flash of teeth in a canine smile before he trotted away, tail wagging behind him. Red followed rather more cautiously, and was pleased to find he'd led her onto a game trail. It was nowhere near as clear as the main path, but there were safe places to step and *slightly* fewer brambles to clutch at her hoodie, so she'd take it.

The forest loomed tall around her, the air damp with trapped moisture and smelling like conifer trees, dirt, and decay. Red loved it in here, loved the moss and lichen, loved the fallen trees slowly turning into soft mulch, their death feeding the life that teemed in every nook and cranny. She wasn't lying when she said these woods were hers, but she also knew deep in her bones that the forest can't belong to *you*. You belong to the forest if it decides to keep you, and Red had always felt kept.

It was a nice hike, easy for the first bit and then switchbacking up the side of a ravine between the ferns and the trees. The last section took all her concentration, because as much as she loved this forest, it was also very much full of shitty rotten holes and slippery fallen branches whose goals in their afterlife appeared to all center around breaking her fucking ankles. The Wolf did his best to lead her on the easiest path, but she still had to scramble up the last ten yards on all fours just for stability.

"There had better not be any more uphill," she panted into the leaf litter. "If you make me go up another ravine I'm gonna—"

Red's voice died in her throat as she looked up, eyes catching on a bright orange, ruffled mushroom just ahead of her, and then another just behind it, and another, and another. She thought she knew all the chanterelle patches in these woods, but this was a new one, and it was *big.* She sat back on her heels, dazed, and everywhere her eyes fell there were more mushrooms, vivid orange standing out against the brown and green like an explosion of flowers. Chanterelles half-hidden under the fall of ferns. Chanterelles poking up from the dirt in little self-made caves of packed, fallen needles. Chanterelles dusted with dirt and leaves and unfurled in the clean, fresh air. This was more chanterelles than she'd ever seen before in her *life,* holy shit.

"Was this..." she started, letting herself trail off as she brushed fallen fir needles off the closest chanterelle. "Was this the surprise?"

The Wolf laid down in the center of the chanterelle patch, careful not to crush any of them, and grinned at her. "It was," he said, sounding immensely smug. "I smelled them coming up after the last rain, and hoped that you would be here when they were ready." He rolled onto his back, belly up, tongue lolling out of his mouth as he looked at her upside-down. "Your timing was excellent."

"So was your nose," Red said, her bewilderment already turning into excitement as she dug a foldable grocery bag out of her backpack. "Do you know how much they sell these for at the farmer's market?"

"No," the Wolf said cheerfully, climbing back to his feet and shaking mulch out of his pelt. "I have no idea how human money works." He picked a few delicate steps closer, almost close enough to touch, and added, "The Witch said you enjoyed them, though. I wanted you to have them."

"Not even God could stop me from taking home these bad boys," she told him gleefully, whipping open her pocketknife with a practiced motion and cutting the stem on the first chanterelle. There were at least—Red did some quick calculations—twenty pounds of mushrooms *just* in this patch. She wouldn't even be able to take all of them with her, so she could focus on the biggest, best ones and come back for the second round in a few days when they'd had more time to grow.

The Wolf sidled up on her, clearly telegraphing his movements so she knew where he was at all times. (He did that as much as possible these days, and it always made Red feel much fonder than she wanted to admit.) "Do they please you, then?" he asked quietly, doing the hilariously bizarre thing where he tried to sound casual and didn't manage it at all. (A wolf pretending to be casual was still the funniest thing in the world to Red, but she kept the amusement to herself.)

"They do," Red answered easily, because who wouldn't be pleased by this many chanterelles? The Wolf said nothing in response, and she glanced up to find his ears barely drooping and his tail almost limp. Was he disappointed? In what?

Wait.

Wait.

Was he disappointed in her *reaction?*

Red looked around at the clearing again, the gorgeous riot of orange and green and brown, and it hit her in slow waves: The Wolf found this for *her.* He listened to her when she told him she liked foraging for mushrooms; he *remembered;* he brought her here because he wanted to show this to *her.* All of this beauty? All of these mushrooms? They were a gift for *her* and her alone.

Had anyone else ever given her something so magical?

Suddenly her response seemed paltry and pathetic. Red set down the knife and the chanterelle, folding her hands in her lap so she could give the Wolf her full attention. "This is beautiful," she said sincerely. "I really love chanterelles, and I'd have to climb all over these ravines and fall in every single fern in this forest if I tried to find these myself, and it was very cool of you to think of me and bring me here." The Wolf's tail was wagging a little, starting to pick up speed, and Red couldn't smother her smile. "Thank you, Wolf."

The Wolf padded a few steps closer, tail wagging in earnest. "I am pleased that you like it," he said, peeking at her out of the corner of his eye almost coquettishly (another expression Red had never thought she'd see on a wolf). "Shall I find you more?" He stood close to her now, closer than any time since that very first day, fur practically vibrating with... *something.*

"Not today," she said, allowing herself to give in to a long-suppressed urge and reaching out a hand to stroke along his shoulders. "There's more here than I can take with me."

The Wolf held perfectly still as her hand moved, like he'd suddenly transformed into a taxidermied replica of himself. It wasn't a bad stillness, though; rather, it was the stillness she sometimes saw in dogs when they were trying with all their might to earn a treat. Her smile grew, a surprising wave of fondness expanding her ribs as she let herself admit something she'd been studiously ignoring: She liked the Wolf. He was gruff, and kind, and dryly funny, and he paid attention to her like she mattered.

"Good boy," she told him, working her fingers into the fur under his ear. "The best boy, aren't you, finding me all these mushrooms."

The Wolf unfroze all at once, tipping his head into her hand so hard his whole body came along for the ride. "I will find you any mushrooms you like," he promised, words half-slurred and his golden eyes closed to slits in absolute bliss. "Any time you like. Anything."

Red got her other hand in there and massaged both his ears at once. "Keep a nose out for morels when we get into spring," she said, the fondness dripping out in her voice now. "I like those just as much as chanterelles."

"I will," the Wolf said, leaning into her touch. "I will."

The Wolf turned out to like chanterelles, too, they found out later, when Red fried some up in butter at her grandma's house and offered him a few through the open door on a spoon.

"Better than the dog treats?" she asked as he licked his chops with every sign of pleasure.

"Better than the crunchy ones," he decided after some careful thought. "Not as good as the little meaty ones."

"Good to know," Red said, and petted his ears.

Red gathered so many chanterelles that year that she almost ran out of room for them in the chest freezer. The Wolf was impossibly smug about this.

The forest shimmered with frost, the path at least thirty percent ice, and the Wolf pressed against her leg as they walked, warming her through her jeans. He listened very intently as Red described the multiple ways in which she both looked forward to and dreaded the upcoming holidays with her family, occasionally making sympathetic noises, and she was so distracted by the conversation that it wasn't until she was walking into her grandma's house and the Wolf came in with her that she realized anything was strange.

"He comes inside now?" she asked her grandma, and then to the Wolf, "You come inside now?"

"If you're cold, they're cold," her grandma called back from the kitchen, poking her head into the entryway. "Bring them inside, that's what the commercials say. Hey, there, Fangs," she added to the Wolf with a wink. "Thanks for lunch."

"Lunch?" Red asked the Wolf with a raised eyebrow as her grandma disappeared back into the kitchen. He blinked at her placidly, big golden eyes wide and guileless.

"It would be rude to impose without bringing a gift," he said eventually in the face of her continued brow-raising. "I planned to visit the Witch today, so I brought her another pheasant." He politely wiped his paws on the mat and padded into the living room, where he flopped down on the rug in front of her grandma's fake electric fireplace and stretched out luxuriously.

"He means I told him you were coming up, and he sprinted into the woods and came back fifteen minutes later with two birds and a sincere request that I cook them for you," Red's grandma yelled, with the same glee she took in telling embarrassing stories about her grandchildren. "I have them in the pressure cooker so we'll have a good stew soon."

"*Really*," Red asked, raising both eyebrows at the Wolf now. "Two birds? How hungry did you think I'd be?"

The Wolf refused to make eye contact, tipping his ears back sheepishly and looking at the fake fireplace instead. "They were small birds," he muttered with a distinctly embarrassed air. "One would have hardly been a gift on its own."

"Whatever you need to tell yourself in order to feel better," Red told him mercilessly, and joined her grandma in the kitchen.

It was really good pheasant.

Red looked out the window at the steadily falling snow and sighed. She was going to have to drive to her grandma's. There was just no way around it. The path turned into a frozen hellscape this time of year (a scenic one, but a frozen hellscape nonetheless), and she knew from experience that trying to climb it would guarantee at least three wipeouts and an icicle nose. She accepted this, and drove in the winter. She had chains in her trunk. It was fine.

Red just wished that maybe she could give someone a heads-up not to expect her at the base of the hill, was all.

Well. No point wallowing. Red shoved her arms into her puffer jacket, loaded up the car with the reusable grocery bags, and headed out. The snow wasn't sticking to the roads yet, but if she stayed at her grandma's past sundown she might as well stay all night because she knew from experience all the slush would turn to ice. She drove carefully but grumpily, internally seething and annoyed about the seething because it was a silly thing to be seething about but she couldn't stop. Her bad mood lasted all the way out along the highway, onto the switchback that took her up the hill, and up the long, winding driveway that led to her grandma's. It lasted right up until she came around the last turn and her headlights (always on this time of year) reflected a familiar yellow flash through the falling snow at the edge of the parking area.

"Wolf," she half-yelled, one leg out of the car and still tangled in her seatbelt. "You were waiting for me?"

"The Witch said the usual path would be inaccessible to you," he said, bounding over and waiting for her to be fully out of the car before winding around her legs. "I thought I should be sure someone was here to greet you when you arrived." The Wolf smiled up at her in his canine way, snowflakes glittering on his gray fur, warm and steady and loyal. Red tried to remember the last time anyone had ever waited for her just to greet her, instead of assuming she was competent enough to take care of things by herself. It had to be while she was still in high school, and she was surprised by how many feelings it brought up.

"Well," she said, forcing her voice to be steady—she could think about feelings later, there was stuff to do right now— "help me get these groceries inside before anything freezes. Or melts. Could go either way."

The Wolf submitted to having the handles of a tote bag slung around his neck and waddled the bag inside with the most bow-legged stance she'd ever seen on an animal. Red laughed into the bright white world and followed him in, heart as light and shining as the snow.

The rain pelted against the windows. Red, who was inside and warm and comfortable in the window seat at her grandma's that overlooked the garden, took another sip of her hot tea and let the rain do what it wanted. She didn't have anywhere to be for at least another hour, and she could drive in the rain with her eyes shut and still get home safely. (Not that she *would,* of course.)

The Wolf, who had jumped up on the other end of the window seat approximately fifteen minutes after she sat down, sighed in a very put-upon way, stretched, and wiggled closer to her lap. He probably thought he was being subtle. Dirtbag the cat *also* thought she was being subtle when she very slowly reached for off-limits food on the table, as though she was invisible to human eyes below a certain speed threshold. (Dirtbag the cat always looked incredibly surprised when she was removed from the situation.)

Neither of them were the least bit subtle, was Red's internal point.

She shifted a little, stretching out her legs on the room-side edge of the bench and leaving a ditch of sorts between herself and the window for the Wolf to ooze into, which he did. He stayed there without moving for a few minutes, then stretched again and "somehow" ended up closer. Red snorted into her tea.

"Just put your damn head in my lap, already," she told him, quietly amused. "We both know that's what you want."

"You have no way of knowing that for sure," the Wolf said, cracking one golden eye to peer up at her. "Perhaps my final goal was to be where I am currently, in this position."

"Perhaps it was…" Red let her voice trail off, then added with an eye roll, "If you were lying to yourself. Just do it."

The Wolf hrumphed at her and did nothing.

Approximately thirty seconds later he hrumphed again and rolled around until he was pressed against her from thighs to calves, his head a heavy, comforting weight across her legs and his body a luxuriously furry line of warmth all the way down. Red immediately felt about three times sleepier than she had been previously. He was just so *cozy.*

"Are you happy with yourself," he asked, eyes shut and voice flat. It rumbled pleasantly against her legs through her sweatpants, and Red's skin went goosebumpy in spite of the warmth.

"I should be asking you the same question," Red told him, and settled a hand between his ears. He sighed in satisfaction when she started scratching, going entirely boneless in that impossible canine way, and Red watched the rain with a small smile she couldn't quite get rid of.

Red's mug of tea was empty and she was giving serious consideration to an *actual* nap when the Wolf sighed hugely, ribcage expanding into her thigh in a strange press-and-release.

"Miss Red," he said quietly, deep voice barely audible. "Thank you."

Red's brow creased. "For?" She really didn't need to be thanked for the petting. She got just as much out of it as he did, she was pretty sure. (The Wolf's ears were *so soft.*)

The Wolf was silent, but she could almost feel him thinking, so she didn't feel ignored. Red kept petting the aforementioned very soft ears while she waited for him to find his words. It took a little while of rain pattering against the window before he finally inhaled again, the air in his lungs pressing them closer for a moment.

"When we first met," he started, sounding as though he was picking his words very carefully, "I was... Unwell." The Wolf paused again, cracking one eye to peek up at her and then directing his gaze toward the room at large. "I had been alone and hungry for a very long time."

"Alone?" Red asked gently, massaging the base of one of his ears.

The Wolf nodded, rubbing his cheek against her pants. "I came here because I was of the age to leave my birth family and find my own pack, but my travels took... much longer than I was expecting, and there was less prey, and it was harder to hunt alone. We wolves are pack animals. We are not meant to be without companions."

Red hummed, still petting him. This was important, she could tell, and she didn't want to interrupt it.

"I did not realize how... unstable I had become until we met." He swallowed and raised his head to regard her solemnly. "I saw you, and you were well-fed and had delicious things with you, and you smelled like you came from a pack, and you were obviously going to visit another member of your pack, and I wanted the pack and the food very desperately, and I... was not in a place to understand that wanting something did not mean I deserved it."

"So you tried to eat me," Red said, letting her smile soften the accusation that would normally accompany the words.

The Wolf gave her a self-deprecating look. "I do not believe I was trying to eat you." His face went distant and thoughtful, the eyebrows he didn't actually have giving the impression of furrowing. "My memory from that time is patchy. I recall the hunger, and the wanting, and the anger at not-having, but I genuinely cannot recall what I thought I was doing when I climbed into the Witch's bed." He paused, and his eyes glinted. "If I had been trying to *actually* eat you, you would have had a harder time fighting me off."

"Says you," Red said, tugging on one of his ears. "You're not scarier than the Browns' shitty untrained Rottweiler."

"I will take your word for it," the Wolf said, looking vaguely offended at being compared to such an animal. He shook himself and looked at her with that solemn, sincere expression again. "All of this is to say, Miss Red, that I know I did not deserve a second chance after my behavior, and every day I am grateful that you were willing to give me one regardless." He stretched up to nose at her cheek gently, just once, and then withdrew as though flustered. "I hold you and the Witch in the highest esteem," he said to the electric fireplace. "Thank you for allowing me to be part of your lives."

Oh, this boy. This fluffy, deadly thing. She'd tried lying to herself about him for a long time, but sometime between the chanterelles and now, Red allowed herself to understand the truth: She liked him. He was probably her best friend in the world, which was maybe a bit sad, but Red had always been too busy to really make friends, so she wasn't going to hold his species against him.

"You know," she started, massaging around his jaw with all her fingers, "if you were a human, we'd call that first day a meet-ugly." Red cupped his broad head in both hands and leaned down to smack a kiss on his forehead. "I like having you around too, you big stinky boy."

"I am not stinky," the Wolf protested, tail thumping against the cushions. "I smell perfectly wonderful."

"Okay, sure," Red agreed easily, kissing each of his velvety ears and settling back into the window seat for a good lounge. "I guess you're okay."

"Hmph," the Wolf said, setting his head happily on her stomach.

"Good boy," Red said, scritching him under his jaw. His tail sped up, beating the cushions like a drum, and she smiled.

Two weeks later Red arrived at her grandma's right before a forecasted ice storm rolled in.

"Oh no," she said, looking out the window at the freezing rain pelting the forest. "I can't drive in this." Her voice had no inflection whatsoever.

"Sure can't," Red's grandma agreed, standing elbow-to-elbow with her at the window. "Guess you'll have to spend the night."

"Guess I will," Red said, still deadpan. "How annoying."

"No one could have predicted this," her grandma said, and patted her shoulder with a wink. "I'll text your mom and let her know."

"You are both doing something strange, and I do not understand what it is or why you are doing it," the Wolf observed from his place on the rug in front of the electric fireplace.

"Don't worry about it," Red told him, getting the kettle on.

"Humans," he muttered to himself, and apparently went to sleep.

Later, after dinner, after an episode of one of the weird British game shows Red's grandma liked to watch and had figured out how to pirate, after Red had changed into a set of pajamas that happened to be in her car and brushed her teeth with the toothbrush she happened to bring with her, she paused at the doorway to the guest bedroom (which no one but Red had slept in for years) and looked at the Wolf.

The Wolf, who by now had commandeered the couch and had spent most of the game show pretending like he wasn't watching Red out of the corner of his eye, looked back at her, head cocked.

Red pushed the bedroom door a little further open and tipped her head inside in invitation.

The Wolf stared at her for a long, silent breath, and oozed off the couch. He practically tiptoed in her direction, as though if he made a sound, she'd change her mind, skirted past her into the room, and—after another assessing look in her direction—jumped up onto the queen-sized bed. He laid down, curling into as small a ball as possible, and peeked at her through his lashes.

"If you do not—"

Red shut the door with a snap. "Shut up."

The Wolf shut up.

Satisfied, Red climbed into bed, plugged in her phone to charge (good thing she happened to have brought her charger), and shut off the light. Outside the wind screamed through the trees, sleet battering the house. Inside everything was quiet. Nothing moved. Red felt entirely alone.

Fuck that.

"How are you supposed to keep me warm if you're way over there?" she complained, rolling onto her side and extending an arm vaguely in the Wolf's direction. "You need to come pay me heat rent."

The Wolf snorted. "Rent is a human concept," he told her, wiggling over until he made contact with her hand and then snuggling up into her as the little spoon. "Also, if I did need to pay rent, it would clearly be to the Witch."

"Shush, you," Red said, already drifting off from the influx of warm, soft wolf cuddle. "G'night."

"Good night," the Wolf said, his voice a low, fond secret, and then Red was asleep.

It was the first truly warm day in spring, sunny and bright after a week of dry, slightly chilly wind, and Red was exactly three steps onto the path to her grandma's when a large gray creature blundered loudly out of the woods, tripped, and crashed into the ground directly in front of her. Red blinked at it in silence. This wasn't how the walk usually started at all.

"Ow," said the creature, in a familiar, unfamiliar voice. It shifted and groaned a little, sounding very longsuffering. "The Witch was right."

Red knew that voice. Red knew that *fur color*. Red did not know that body shape (bipedal) or those clothes (a pair of black culotte pants and a gray t-shirt), but there was only one conclusion she could draw, no matter how confusing: "Wolf?"

The Wolf (for it had to be the Wolf) rolled over onto his back and offered her a sheepish canine smile. "I had intended this to be a surprise."

"Well, I'm fucking surprised," Red said faintly. The Wolf was not a wolf anymore, except for all the ways in which he was still a wolf. He had fur and golden eyes, ears pricked forward and great sharp teeth in his muzzle. He had a tail (she'd seen it before he rolled over) and large, broad paws on his backward-kneed back legs.

He *also* had broad human shoulders, and a mane of longer charcoal hair falling from his head down the back of his neck, and—and *arms* and *hands*.

Red found herself sitting on the path without consciously deciding to do so. Her knees felt like jelly. She had both hands in her hair, because if she didn't have something to hold on to, she was pretty sure she'd float away from reality entirely.

"Hey, Wolf," she said. "What the fuck?"

The Wolf snorted and rolled awkwardly onto all fours, and then crawled to her with enviable grace. (*Of course,* Red thought wildly. *He's more used to four legs.*) He carefully (if a little clumsily) pulled her hands away from her hair and held them in his. (Hands! His hands!!!)

"Good afternoon, Miss Red," he said warmly, brushing his thumbs(!) over her knuckles. "I have learned the magic required to turn myself into a human."

Red stared at him. "*Have* you?" she asked in a near-shriek.

The Wolf rumbled an amused sound and looked down at himself. "Not entirely," he allowed. "But you must admit I am much closer to human form than I was previously."

"That's... true." How were they having a normal conversation about this. What the fuck. "Grandma said you needed more practice?" her mouth asked without waiting for input from her brain.

The Wolf nodded, his ears drooping a bit. "With walking on two legs," he clarified. "It is... challenging."

"Yeah, well, I trip sometimes too. You're not alone." There were two Reds, she decided, the one saying things very casually and then the one having a screaming panic attack in the back of her brain. Good that there were two of them, or the panic attack would be the one in charge. "Wait, can you change *back?*" How was he supposed to hunt if he couldn't move well on two legs? He'd starve! He'd fall down a ravine in the forest and break his leg and he'd *die!*

The Wolf deflated slightly, his shoulders pulling in and his ears drooping further. "Are you not pleased by my appearance? I thought... The Witch said..."

"No, you look—you look fine—" *Weirdly hot, actually*, said the part of Red's brain that had imprinted on Disney's *Robin Hood* at a young age "—but how—"

The Wolf perked up at "fine," which was a seriously weak compliment, and she heard his tail thump the ground a couple of times. "The Witch helped me," he said, answering *an* unasked-question but not the one she was freaking out about. "There were many steps, and it took longer than I had expected." He paused and scrutinized her carefully, eyebrows (and they were much more like real eyebrows now) scrunching in. "If you are not displeased by my appearance, then why are you so agitated?"

"How are you going to *hunt?*" Red blurted. Why was she the only one focusing on the real issue, here? "I'm gonna have to bring you *so many* dog treats until you figure out how your legs work!"

The Wolf laughed, a booming sound that seemed to rattle the trees. His smile was somewhere between canine and human when he finally met her eyes again. Red's hand jerked toward it (maybe if she touched it, things would feel real) but got nowhere because—ah, yes—they were still holding hands. Because the Wolf had hands now.

"I am still capable of taking my original form," he told her soothingly, the corners of his eyes pinching up with amusement. "This is an addition, not a trade."

"Good. Good." Red held onto his hands like he was the last good tomato at the farmer's market and someone was going to try to take him away from her. (If she treated an actual tomato like this she'd destroy it, but the Wolf was made of tougher stuff.) "I'm glad you're not going to starve."

The Wolf laughed again—a distressingly lovely sound—and gave her a fond look. "I trust that, were I to be unable to hunt for an extended period of time, you would not allow me to starve."

Well, that was true, but the Wolf didn't have to go *saying* it.

Red was still struggling for a response when the Wolf squeezed her hands and added, "I would like to show you something before you visit the Witch."

"Is it more mushrooms?" Red asked, allowing the Wolf to pull her to her feet (easily, too, which was saying something—Red wasn't a small woman) and steadying him when he immediately wobbled. They'd gone morel hunting a few weeks previously, and it had been a productive hunt, but she was pretty sure they were outside that season now.

"It is a surprise," the Wolf said with an air of mystery that was somewhat damaged when he went to take a step, waved an arm wildly, and crashed into Red's side as she ducked in to keep him upright. "My forelegs do not know what they are doing," he grumbled into her hair.

"This—" Red patted his back and tried not to focus on how warm and muscular he felt "—wasn't *enough* of a surprise?" Was he trying to kill her? "And they're called arms."

"Arms," the Wolf repeated, like he was committing it to memory. He probably was. "This surprise is related to the other surprise," he continued, leaning heavily on her elbow as he took a few more wobbly steps. "I wanted us to walk there together."

"And how's that going for you?" Red asked, somewhere between sarcastic and sincere.

"Less well than I had hoped," the Wolf admitted, hobbling along with her assistance. "I thought the Witch was exaggerating when she said how long it would take to get used to two legs."

"How far away is your surprise?" Red set aside the question of her grandma's involvement for the moment (though she was going to have a *lot* of pointed questions for her grandma later) in favor of focusing on the practical issues at hand. (Or foot. Or paw, as the case might be.)

"It took perhaps fifteen minutes in my original form?" the Wolf said, a bit uncertainly. "I am still not entirely clear how your human timekeeping works."

Red did some mental math. Given that they'd managed maybe ten yards of movement in the past five minutes... "Okay, no, that's going to take forever. Just switch back and show me where we're going."

The Wolf drooped a bit. "So you *are* displeased with this form."

"No, I just want us to get to your other surprise before we both die of old age," Red said with an expressive eye roll. She glanced down at his t-shirt and frowned. "Wait, did you wear that in wolf form?"

"No," the Wolf said, almost insulted. "I carried them here in my mouth and put them on when I changed form."

"Great, then we'll just do that the other way." She patted his arm and stepped away, making sure he kept his balance while she gave him room to shift. "Switch back."

The Wolf seemed like he wanted to grumble about it some more, but he obeyed anyway, shaking out the mane around his neck and—there wasn't an actual *shift,* not like in the werewolf movies. He was simply a wolf-man one moment and a wolf the next, without any kind of stop in the middle. Red felt like she'd blinked, but she hadn't *actually* blinked. It was more like the world had blinked *around* her.

It was *weird.*

"Ah," the Wolf said from inside his t-shirt, which he was attempting to remove with his back legs, which were themselves entangled in his culottes. "I may have done that in the wrong order."

"It's a new skill," Red said, dropping into a crouch and helping him out of the clothes. "You'll get better at it." *Since you can turn into a wolf-man now!* the panicked voice in the back of her head screamed, not happy at being ignored. Red kept ignoring it. It could get used to being unhappy.

"I appreciate your faith in me," the Wolf said in a long-suffering tone as she wiggled him out of the culottes in an incredibly undignified manner. Once free of his self-inflicted cloth prison, he rolled to his feet and shook himself until his fur all pointed in the correct directions again. "This way."

Red tucked his clothes into her ever-present backpack and followed him off the path. It took maybe twenty minutes to get to the second surprise—the Wolf wasn't always great at judging distances where human strides were concerned—and he took her on such an unfamiliar route that Red had no idea where they were going until they came around a massive old tree and the waterfall opened up in front of them.

Red drifted to a stop just to take in the view. She loved this waterfall, for all that she didn't visit it that frequently these days. It wasn't huge, wasn't anything that would show up on maps, but it was *hers,* a secret place she used to escape to as a child. The falls were maybe twenty feet high, tumbling down a fern-crusted rock face into a surprisingly deep pool (good for swimming only in high summer, otherwise you'd freeze your tits off) and babbling off through the woods in an easily-waded creek. The trees opened up here around a collection of large, flat boulders that Red assumed had been deposited when a glacier melted some hundreds of thousands of years ago, letting the sun stream into the clearing and throw rainbows in the spray at the base of the falls. She *loved* it here.

The Wolf trotted to the smooth plane of the largest boulder and sat down on a blanket? Next to a... Was that a cooler? He waited there for her, tail wagging wildly and his golden eyes bright with anticipation.

"What's this?" Red asked, hauling herself up after him.

"The Witch tells me it is called a 'picnic,'" he said with absolute seriousness. "I asked why you had a specific word for eating outside in the woods, and she said that people who take *all* their meals outside in the woods wouldn't understand such things."

"She does have a point," Red said, halting next to the blanket while her mind reeled. A picnic? For her? For *them?*

"It seemed a fair point," the Wolf agreed, and fidgeted a bit. "May I have my clothes back, please?"

Red set them on the ground where he could reach them and turned her back, trying to focus on the waterfall and not the shifting sounds and quiet curses coming from behind her. The Wolf was naked normally, she told herself. He was covered in fur! He was a wolf! There was no reason she should be standing here, acutely aware that if she turned around, she might catch a glimpse of the Wolf sans clothing.

He didn't have pecs before, a horrible little voice in the back of her mind pointed out. Red mentally gave the voice the finger.

"Ready," he said, in his deeper, human(ish) voice, and Red tried to mentally prepare herself before she turned around. Nope! Still weird! Still weird to see her Wolf in, like, werewolf form, mid-transformation with broad shoulders that stretched the seams of his t-shirt. Which he was wearing. Because if he was naked *now* it would be weird.

Red *really* needed to stop thinking about the Wolf being naked.

"How did you get all this down here?" she asked, desperate for a distraction.

"I carried it," the Wolf said proudly, waving her to a seat on the blanket and opening the cooler with carefully rehearsed movements.

"How?"

"I packed everything into the cooler, and then I carried the cooler in my mouth," the Wolf admitted, pulling out a couple of tupperware containers and then a thermos. "I thought it was better not to attempt the hike on two legs for the first time *while* carrying a cooler, though I can see how it would be more convenient to be able to use my hands for something like that."

"Hands are pretty great." Wow, Red felt so smart and articulate today. Like, yes, extenuating circumstances (The wolf!!! A man!!!) but she didn't particularly enjoy sounding like a toddler who only recently acquired language.

"I am finding them more versatile than paws," the Wolf said sincerely, so maybe he just didn't have a lot of conversational experience outside of Red and her grandma and this still seemed normal to him. "I would not have been able to make these before I took this form."

"Make?" Red asked, and then looked at his hands(!) where he was cracking open a tupperware with a minimum of fumbling. He got the lid open immediately after she spoke, freeing a waft of savory, spicy *something* to float on the air, something familiar that set her mouth watering. "Wait," she said, all the weirdness about the Wolf's shoulders and hands suddenly forgotten. "Wait, are those—"

"Chipotle-cheddar scones," the Wolf said, enunciating the words carefully. "The Witch said they were your favorite."

Red blinked hard several times, but her eyes weren't lying: The tupperware was full of ugly, inexpertly shaped, delicious smelling baked goods.

"You can't eat these," her mouth said, not waiting for input from her brain. *Someone* had to keep canines from getting liver damage, and as usual, the task fell to Red.

"The Witch thinks I may be able to digest alliums in this form," the Wolf said, head slightly cocked. "She said she needed to do more research." He shook himself and pushed the tupperware closer. "It is irrelevant, though. I do not intend to eat these. I made them for you."

Okay, the allium thing was potentially a relief, but: "You made these?" Red asked, her voice ticking higher with each word.

"The Witch helped," the Wolf said earnestly. "There were many steps I was unfamiliar with. She also taught me how to use a knife." He opened the second tupperware to reveal the least consistently sized fruit salad Red had ever seen in her life. "I need more practice," he admitted, "but the Witch said that since I did not cut myself, it counted as a success."

"It's a good guideline," Red agreed distantly, heart pounding so hard she was going a little lightheaded. She reached a shaking hand for one of his and clutched it like she was hanging from a helicopter in an action movie. (There was enough adrenaline in her for it.) "Wolf. I'm going to ask you a question."

The Wolf turned to face her, ears pricked up and his handsome face attentive. Fuck. His face was handsome. *Fuck.* "Yes?" he asked when she had a slight freakout over that realization and stayed silent for too long.

Right. Okay. "Why did you decide you wanted to take this form?"

The Wolf flicked his ears in a nervous tell, but his voice was steady and his eyes were warm when he said, "Because I could not remain a wolf."

Red squinted at him suspiciously. "That's not the full answer."

"No," the Wolf admitted a bit sheepishly. He flicked his ears again. "I could not remain a wolf, Miss Red, because I could not court you as a wolf."

Cool. Red was going to pass out. "Court me?" She heard him just fine, the issue was making herself actually process the words.

The Wolf nodded, his gaze still incredibly earnest. "I needed to be in a form that you could see as worthy," he said, thumb caressing her knuckles. "It did not matter how many pheasants I hunted for you and how many mushroom patches I led you to if I was in a form that would not allow us to be together."

Red nodded, every inch of her body coming up in nervous goosebumps. "And when you say 'together…'"

The Wolf swallowed visibly and dropped his gaze down to their joined hands. "I wish for us to be mates," he said, voice low, eyes flicking up and away like a flash of light from golden jewelry. "Or the human term is… Lovers? I would be the 'boyfriend'?" He pronounced it strangely, like he was learning the language for the first time. It was really, really cute.

"Okay," Red said, nodding again like a bobblehead going over a gravel road. "Great. Thank you for explaining." She patted his hand and then turned to the tupperware, carefully closing the lids, stacking them and the thermos back in the cooler, and closing up the cooler. She was aware of the weight of the Wolf's eyes on her the whole time and did not allow it to make her speed up. It was very important to put the food away. The *most* important.

As soon as the lid clicked shut on the cooler, Red whipped around and *launched* herself at the Wolf. He caught her with a surprised, "Ooof!" that she immediately muffled.

With her mouth.

Kissing a muzzle was a *little* weird, but not weirder than kissing a regular human's mouth was (kissing was just weird no matter how you sliced it, in Red's opinion) and the Wolf had more lip control in this form (and more lip in general) than he had as a regular wolf, so it wasn't a bad kiss overall. It was, however, quite probably the Wolf's first kiss, so Red pulled away after a moment to give him a chance to actually react.

"Was that a yes?" he asked after a long, gobsmacked moment where all he could manage was blinking.

"Yes," Red said firmly, arranging herself more comfortably in his lap and getting her hands into his mane. "I reserve kissing for boyfriends." (This was partly a lie—Red had more hookups under her belt than actual boyfriends, but she wasn't about to waste time right now by laying out her entire dating history.)

"Oh." The Wolf cocked his head at her, a warm delight spreading across his face. "Then can we do it again?"

Red kissed him rather than answering with words, making it a little less desperate this time. The Wolf made a pleased rumble deep in his chest and matched her movements, hesitantly setting his hands on her back where they spread out large and warm over the worn material of her red hoodie. Hmm. No. The hoodie didn't need to be part of this, Red decided, and she unzipped it and wiggled it off without breaking the kiss, which meant the Wolf's big paw-like hands petted down her spine with only her thermal between their skin, which was *very* good. Red shivered and gasped, unintentionally breaking the kiss, and the

Wolf nosed under her jaw and tentatively flicked his tongue at her earlobe.

"You can do that again," Red said, trying not to yank the Wolf's mane too hard while also keeping his mouth exactly where it was via mane-gripping. The Wolf huffed another pleased sound—less of a rumble, more of a snort this time—and traced his tongue along the line of her jaw, and then licked all the way up her jugular. Red shivered again, harder this time, and abandoned the Wolf's mane to yank at the hem of his shirt.

It took the Wolf a moment to figure out what she was doing (probably because he didn't usually wear shirts or make out with humans, so he didn't understand the social cues) but when he figured it out he did his best to help remove it. This meant, functionally, that it took three times as long to get it off as it should have, because he kept blundering his hands into hers and knocking her off-track. (Red very kindly did not laugh at him when he somehow got stuck with his head and one arm in the same hole, but she *did* absolutely file it away later so she could make fun of him for it when he was generally better at wearing clothing.)

The Wolf ended up shirtless, though, which was the important thing, and Red sat back on his lap and petted her hands over his collarbones and shoulders, marveling at the warm, soft feel of him. How did the magic work, she wondered? Did he get to choose the form he ended up with, or did the magic simply turn him into the human(ish) version of himself? As a wolf he was on the larger size of average, his build filled out from a year of regular meals and hours spent roaming the forest. As a human he was broad-shouldered and thick-thighed, muscle apparent under the soft fur and fat padding his frame. Red didn't know if she specifically had a type, really, but the Wolf wasn't *not* it.

The fur on his chest and belly was finer and softer than the fur of his mane and shorter, almost like velvet. She traced her fingers over his velvet-furred torso, down to the waistband of his pants and then back up his obliques, lightly over his pecs and down the line of his arms. The velvet fur texture continued where all the tenderest places on a human would be, the insides of his wrists and arms warm to the touch where his skin was closer to the air. It was also sensitive, to judge by the quiet, panting whines the Wolf made as she explored. Red spread both her hands over his pecs and squeezed, both because she wanted to see what it felt like and because she wanted to see his reaction.

The Wolf whined louder this time, hands jumping to her hips as he tossed his head back. Yep. That was a good reaction. Red decided that it wasn't fair if he was the only shirtless one, and stripped off her thermal with brusque efficiency. The Wolf gaped at her, which was honestly hilarious because she'd never seen a wolf *gape* before. He looked like her chub rolls and her sweaty, worn-out cotton sports bra were the best things he'd ever seen in his life, and his hands reverently drifted up from her hips to cup her love handles. She might have considered feeling self-conscious about that, except the Wolf followed it by doing a sit up that made his abs stand out under his fur and padding and chose to end it by burying his face in her cleavage.

He inhaled there and whined again on the exhale, hands roaming her back, and Red took the opportunity to massage his ears, scratching deeply into the fur around them. The Wolf rumbled, almost like he was trying to purr, and raised his head out of her tits to look at her in something like awe.

"How can I please you?" he asked, much more earnestly than any of Red's previous partners had ever even considered asking anything similar to that question. She considered her options. What *did* she actually want? She hadn't thought making out with a hot wolf man was on the menu for today. It was a pleasant surprise, to be sure, but now Red had to make some actual decisions about where things were going to go.

Did she want to fuck the hot wolf man right now?

Red looked down at the Wolf, at his wide golden eyes and dark pupils, the open admiration on his face, his broad shoulders and big hands.

Yes. She wanted to fuck the hot wolf man. She one hundred percent wanted to fuck the hot wolf man right now. (For a given value of fuck. She didn't have any condoms with her, and she wasn't about to risk a wolf baby before she knew if that was a possibility they had to worry about.)

"You should take your pants off," she said decisively. "And help me take mine off, too."

The Wolf licked his chops and swallowed, a fine tremor in his hands where they reflexively squeezed her hips. "Yes," he said, more of a breath than anything, and went for her fly.

This was a disaster, as the Wolf had clearly never attempted to navigate a button before, to say nothing of a zipper. Red rolled off him to the side and wiggled her jeans down over her ass while he worked on her boots. He managed the laces admirably, scrabbling her boots off and watching avidly while she kicked her jeans away.

"Your pants, too," she ordered, yanking her sports bra off over her head and only momentarily getting stuck in it. When she escaped its elastic clutches, the Wolf was frozen, staring at her tits like he wanted to pound on a table and yell, "*AWOOGA!*" It was very flattering.

His fucking pants were still on.

"I gotta do everything myself around here," Red half-complained, getting her fingers under his waistband and pulling. That snapped him out of it, and between the two of them they managed to get the culottes off without tearing anything or yanking the Wolf's tail uncomfortably. Red checked before she put them aside and, as expected, the hole for the Wolf's tail showed clear signs of having been carefully torn open at the center back seam and then hemmed with neat stitches. She was going to have to have a conversation with her grandma about this conspiracy.

The Wolf whined for her attention, nosing at the line of her shoulder, and Red was going to have a conversation with her grandma *later*. She threw the culottes on top of her abandoned hoodie and turned back to the Wolf, eager to get her hands all over him in general and on one specific part of him in particular. (She was also incredibly curious about that specific part of him, which she thought was extremely reasonable. She'd never fucked a hot wolf man before. She didn't know where that was going to land between "wolf" and "man," and the answer was going to be very relevant to her very soon.)

The Wolf caught Red easily when she launched herself at him, wrapping his arms around her and tucking his muzzle into the crook of her neck. He inhaled deeply there and exhaled with a shudder, fingertips flexing against her lower back. "You smell so *good*," he told her like it was a secret prayer. Red shivered at the sincerity in his voice, and then again when he licked her neck. "How can I please you?" he repeated, still in that low, wanting voice. Red didn't know what to do with this level of sexy devotion all pointed in her direction. She felt practically drunk with it.

She *could* at least answer his question, though, and she found his wrists, guiding his hands to her breasts and showing him how to cup her. "Circles around the nipples," she said, aware of her blush and deciding to actively ignore it. "You can pinch them a little, but gently."

The Wolf nodded, staring intently at his hands as he kneaded her tits experimentally. "I read that many humans enjoy mouth stimulation as well?"

Red shuddered at the thought, and also because he was dragging a thumb around one tight nipple. "I sure do," she said, and then, "Wait, you *read* it? Where?" She blinked, another question popping up. "You know how to read?"

The Wolf gave her a wounded look. "I have been *learning*," he said, slightly offended. "Did you not think me capable?"

"I didn't think you had books in the woods," Red said, which she thought was reasonable.

"Not typically," the Wolf admitted, "though I did occasionally find caches of very particular kinds of magazines." His nose wrinkled. "I do not understand why one would store such things in a hollow log."

"No one really knows," Red assured him, arching as he got the other thumb into the action, too. "It's just one of those things."

"I did not see the point of such magazines previously," the Wolf said, attempting some careful pinching, which Red felt tingle in her low back and her scalp and—most importantly—her pussy. "Ah," he said in tones of satisfied understanding, "you enjoy that."

"What gave it away?" Red asked, half-joking, as though she wasn't squirming on his lap trying to get friction on her clit, tits pressed into his hands like they belonged there. She wasn't expecting an answer, so she didn't understand what was happening right away when the Wolf leaned in to nuzzle at her collarbone, tracing his nose up the line of her neck to her ear with a long, slow inhale.

"Your scent," he murmured in her ear, tongue flicking out to taste her earlobe. "You smell more intense when I do something you like."

Red hid her face in the Wolf's mane, feeling herself flush all the way down her neck. "Oh, god, you can *smell* when I'm horny?"

The Wolf chuckled and kissed under her ear. "Among other things," he admitted. "I like all the ways you smell." He teased her nipples with the edges of his fingernails, licking along her neck at the same time, and Red made the kind of sound she previously thought was made up for porn. He hummed smugly and licked the other side of her neck. "You *do* enjoy mouths."

"As previously established," Red grumbled, distracted by everything happening with her tits and also the hot pressure of something very hard against the back of one thigh. Oh, fuck, she was about to ask for something that a year ago would have seemed impossible, but she sure wanted it now. "You can use your teeth?"

The Wolf froze. "What?"

Red squeezed her eyes shut, wondering what exactly he could read from her scent right now. "Bite me a little," she said as confidently as she could. "I'm into it."

The Wolf exhaled against her neck. "You are sure?"

Red bit her lower lip, trying to center herself as much as possible while sitting on a hot wolf man's dick with his hands on her tits. Was she sure? "Yes," she said after a deep breath. "Yes, I trust you."

The Wolf sighed, his breath coming out uneven, and he carefully—*so carefully*—grazed the line of her jugular with his fangs. Red shivered all the way down to her tailbone at the sharp scrape of it, so delicate it almost tickled. Beyond the physical sensation was the mental, a sharp terror deep in her hindbrain fighting with the desire aching in her body. He could kill her with a single bite, she knew this, and she also knew he *wouldn't*. It was a potent combination, one that had Red moaning and arching her neck to get him to do it again.

The Wolf made a pleased, relieved sound and very gently nibbled her earlobe. "I read that some humans enjoyed biting, but I did not think it wise to assume that would apply to you." His tongue flicked out as though to soothe the bite (not that he was biting so hard that Red needed soothing) and added, "Or that it would include biting from me."

"Yeah, well," Red said distractedly, what with how he was nipping along her jawline now, "guess we're both learning new things today." All of the sexy biting wasn't quite enough to distract her from the ping of a previous question resurfacing, and she tugged the Wolf's mane. "Where did you read all this?"

The Wolf leaned away to make somewhat sheepish eye contact. (She got the impression that he'd be blushing, if he could.) "Several places," he said, a bit cagily. "The Witch showed me how to use the internet, and suggested some resources where I might find useful information."

Oh, Red was going to have *such* a talk with her grandma. "Did you look at *porn?*"

The Wolf gave her an affronted look. "I did *research,*" he said primly, "at places that purported to be educational. I do not believe that counts as what you humans consider pornography."

Okay, Red had to admit he had a point. She decided to ignore that point in favor of tugging on his mane again and kissing the hinge of his jaw. "You wanna show me what you learned, then, so I can be the judge of how educational it was?"

The Wolf a) growled and b) tackled her backward onto the picnic blanket, a hand tucked behind her head to protect it from the impact, so Red figured that was probably a yes. He also licked a broad stripe over one entire fucking tit before sucking on her nipple like it was the only way to save her from a fairy-tale curse, so that was also a pretty significant clue. It was messy, and hot, and very tongue-forward (which wasn't surprising when Red thought about it, not that she had much mental energy to spare for thinking about it), and by the time the Wolf made it to the waistband of her underwear, they were both panting and whining almost in unison.

"May I—" the Wolf started, sounding like *he* was the one who'd just had his nipples sucked on until his entire body was ready to launch off the earth and into orbit.

"Yes, yes, do it," Red ordered, shoving down her underwear and narrowly avoiding kicking the Wolf in the jaw as she scrambled them off. She took a moment to wish she'd worn something slightly nicer than a pair of faded black boyshorts, but it wasn't like the Wolf had opinions about human fashion. Also, as soon as she was fully naked, the Wolf dove into her fucking pussy tongue-first like if he waited even another *second* they'd both explode.

Red made a sound that probably frightened several nearby birds, her hands coming down to land on the Wolf's ears. She had just enough brainpower to move her hands to just *behind* his ears before she grabbed on, two fistfuls of his mane clamped in her white-knuckled fingers. He threw her legs over his shoulders easily, like they weighed nothing, his hands wrapped around her sturdy thighs from the outside to keep them spread, like she might try to do something to stop him in his enthusiastic pussy-eating efforts. Red had no plans to stop him. Red had plans to come in possibly the next thirty seconds if everything continued as it was. She was very much in favor of this, actually.

The Wolf made a sound somewhere between a growl and a moan as he ate her out, which vibrated into Red's body and prickled across her skin. She'd enjoyed oral before, sure, but it was never like this, so all-consuming and *focused*. Also, she'd never been eaten out by a hot wolf-man before, so there were several new experiences she was dealing with at the same time.

"Oh," she gasped, abs tense and her back arching up off the rock beneath her. "Oh—fuck—*Wolf*—" and she came like getting caught in a landslide. Her vision whited out, and she trembled in every single limb with her hands so tight in the Wolf's mane she worried vaguely and distantly about whether she was hurting him. She didn't have the capacity to really focus on the worry, though, too busy trying to remember to breathe while her pussy clenched on nothing and her hips rode the Wolf's face with an instinctive urgency. When she was finally aware of things other than pleasure again her entire body tingled like a limb waking up from being asleep, only in a very good way instead of being annoying and painful.

"Wow," she said, lightheaded. Oh, breathing would probably be good, huh? Red did some of that.

"Did I please you?" the Wolf asked earnestly. When Red gathered the bodily control to look down at him, she found him with his cheek pressed to the inside of one thigh and his golden eyes so dilated they were practically black. He licked his chops in evident pleasure as he petted the outside of one of her legs in long, soothing swipes, and seemed like he'd be happy to stay there for the rest of the day. (He also seemed like he didn't care about her leg hair in the slightest. Given the state of his own leg hair—fur—this made sense, but was still very flattering in a weird, stomach-fluttery way.)

"You pleased me so good I don't know if I can move my legs," Red said, managing to get her hands in gear to scritch behind his ears. He made a pleased whuffing sound and pressed into her touch, eyes drifting half shut. It was cute. He was very cute. Red could almost fall asleep here on a sun-warmed rock, naked in the forest, especially if he kept cuddling her like this.

Red didn't want to fall asleep, though.

Red wanted to see the Wolf's dick.

And touch it, to be clear. There was going to be touching.

"Come here," Red ordered, her plan starting to take shape. She tugged on his ears until he got the message and crawled up her body for a hug, and then she rolled him onto his back with the kind of sharp, controlled movement that had served her well on the wrestling team in high school. The Wolf sprawled out on the blanket with a surprised little yip, and Red pushed herself up onto one elbow, trying to get the lay of the land, as it were. She also put her hand on his belly, because sometimes to get the lay of the land, you need to feel it.

"Miss Red," the Wolf panted, looking at her almost in a panic. "You—you—what?"

"Just Red," she said, petting his belly in soothing sweeps and getting a good feel for his abs at the same time. Yes, the touching was an excellent choice.

"Red," he said on a groan, turning his muzzle into his arm and hiding it there, hips hitching up. "Red, you do not have to—"

"I want to," Red told him, leaning over to kiss him on the cheek as she let her hand wander a little lower. "Don't you want me to? Aren't I allowed to want to please *you?*"

The Wolf made a pitiful whining sound, peeking out from behind his arm. Red kissed him between the eyes, pausing her hand where she was pretty sure she could feel the heat from whatever a hot wolf-man packed between his legs. "Do you want it?" she asked in his ear, lips brushing the sensitive shell of it. "Can I touch you?"

The Wolf made another one of those pitiful, needy sounds. He audibly swallowed and then nodded, abs trembling under her hand and his whole body twitching with the aborted need to move.

"Good boy," Red said, giving him another kiss on the ear, and he fucking *bucked* like they were suddenly at a rodeo. It was quite a reaction, and Red took careful note of it for later as she slid her hand further down and it finally brushed against something hot and unfurred. Jackpot.

Red thought sometimes that actively looking at someone's dick seemed... rude, maybe? She knew this was a silly thing to think—if you look at the rest of someone's body, there's no reason not to look at their dick, too, plus sometimes you needed to look at it to see what you were doing! Today, with the Wolf, and with *this* particular dick? She felt none of that hesitation. She kissed the Wolf's ear again and looked down the line of his body as she wrapped her hand around it. There were some genuine and practical anatomical questions that needed answering, but more importantly? Red just wanted to look.

A tiny thread of anxiety in the back of Red's mind disappeared almost immediately, because the Wolf's dick was—generally speaking—human. It looked like maybe there was a sheath at the base, so when he wasn't aroused it wouldn't be visible (a piece of evolutionary design Red often thought would have been nice to carry over into humanity, not that anyone asked her opinion) but the shaft of it was smooth and velvet-hard. It felt like a perfectly normal dick, proportionate to the Wolf's size (Red's cervix gave a sigh of relief), flushed dark with bloodflow and leaking from the tip. Red gave it a slow pump with her hand, slightly distracted with questions about whether the lack of foreskin was normal or not, but the way the Wolf flung his head back and whine-howled into the sky quickly took precedence.

"Shh," she said, cuddling closer and adding a twist at the top on her next stroke, smearing the Wolf's precome around with careful precision. "Don't worry, my Wolf. I'll take care of you."

The Wolf made another incoherent sound, possibly past language, and Red smothered her smirk as she worked him over. She was used to men who behaved as though making noise in bed was somehow unmanly, which probably explained why she hadn't dated any of them for very long. The Wolf appeared to have missed that memo (and probably every other memo—the forest was not known to receive many memos in general), because he panted and whined and moaned through his teeth, one arm wrapped behind her back to hold her close as he writhed against the very rumpled blanket.

"Red," he begged, pressing his face to her collarbones and trembling through his entire body. "Red, please, will you—" His voice broke off into another whine when she rubbed her thumb in a circle right under the head of his dick, inspiring another round of leaking.

"Will I what?" Red asked, absolutely drunk on power at having such a deadly, dangerous creature begging for pleasure in her arms.

The Wolf panted and licked her throat, every exhale almost a word. "Will you say it?" he pleaded, sounding entirely undone. "Will you call me—please?"

Ah. *Aha.* Red felt something feral and satisfied growl deep in her chest. She held the Wolf—*her* Wolf close, hand buried in his mane, and tightened her grip on the upstroke.

"*Good boy.*"

The Wolf came with a howl, dick pulsing in her hand as he emptied himself onto his belly. Red made soothing sounds and jerked him through it, eyes locked on the subsequent mess and honestly fairly impressed. She stopped when his shaking turned into a flinch and then just held him gently, letting him soften under the weight of her palm while he panted for breath. He kept whining on the exhale, but now it seemed to be from overwhelm instead of from neediness. (It was very cute, regardless.)

"How was that?" she couldn't help asking. "Good for you?"

"I did not know you were being literal about your legs, earlier," the Wolf said roughly, still panting. He nuzzled into her neck and breathed there, nose just touching her collarbone. "Thank you," he murmured, a barely-there rumble. "Red. My mate."

Red felt herself flush all the way down to her tits. "You're welcome," she said awkwardly. This was maybe a little too sincere a conversation to have while she still had her hand on the Wolf's dick. She kissed the top of his head anyway. "Come on, my Wolf. Let's clean you up."

The Wolf made a questioning sound when she reached for her backpack with her clean hand, intent on finding some tissues or something. Red hummed acknowledgment of his question, and the Wolf cleared his throat.

"Can I not simply lick it?" he asked, sounding both like he thought this was the most logical thing to do and also like he would not be surprised to hear it was against the rules of human sex.

Red paused. Actually, it really *was* the most logical thing, and—in spite of what some straight men seemed to think—wasn't actually against any rules of human sex, so... "If you want?"

The Wolf gave a satisfied little huff and suited actions to words, starting with Red's hand before moving on to the rest of the mess, which was... okay, wow, he was *flexible* and Red had some *thoughts* about that. They were thoughts that would have to wait for another time, though, and she reached for her underwear and pants with determination.

There was still a picnic to eat, after all.

The chipotle cheddar scones were so good Red might have ended up crying a little, but the Wolf's shoulder was there for her to cry on, so that was fine. It was just—he made them! For *her!*

The walk back to Red's grandma's house took much longer than it normally would have, because the Wolf insisted on doing it in his mostly-human form so he could practice, and he kept tripping on things. It took less time than it could have, though, because Red insisted on carrying the much-lighter cooler so the Wolf could use his arms for balance. They made it out of the woods as the afternoon tipped into evening, and Red's grandma opened the door before they needed to knock.

"Welcome back," she told the Wolf, and then, "You're welcome," she told Red.

"We are going to have a conversation about your meddling," Red said with extreme dignity.

"I meddled some condoms and some lube into the nightstand in your room," Red's grandma said with a horrible grin, "so when we have that conversation, remember to thank me, too."

"I hate you," Red said, and breezed into the house while her grandma laughed until she started coughing.

They did make use of the condoms later, when Red pinned the Wolf to the bed and rode him until he howled, one hand on his shoulder for balance and the other rubbing her clit until she came, possibly making her own howling sound in the process. Just because Red's grandma was a horrible, evil meddler didn't mean Red was going to look gift condoms in the mouth, or something.

After (the howling, and the cleanup) Red lay on her back with the Wolf curled into her side, head pillowed on the place where her shoulder met her chest. It didn't escape her notice that this meant he was basically laying his head to rest on her titty. She didn't begrudge him this—she had nice tits, and was pleased to have them thus appreciated. Also, she found it very cute that he seemed to be trying to make himself as small as possible, like a pit mix that desperately wanted to be a lap dog.

"Red?" he asked quietly into the satisfied darkness, thumb playing over the jut of her bare hip bone. "Would it please you to name me?"

Red opened her eyes, suddenly very awake. "Do you *want* me to name you?"

The Wolf hesitated, a tension in his frame. "Humans name things," he said, which wasn't entirely an answer. Red scritched behind his ear and waited for the rest of the explanation. It took a while before the Wolf inhaled again and said carefully, "If you named me, I would be yours."

"Aren't you already?" Red asked, voice gentle. She could tell this was important, and didn't want to fuck it up.

The Wolf hesitated again. Red took a slow breath and willed her heart rate down. They didn't *both* need to be nervous. "I am bound to you," he said eventually, each word precise, "but you have not claimed me."

Oh. *Oh.* Red understood in a flash, everything coming into perfect, crystal clarity. Now it was her turn to figure out what to say, and she kissed the top of the Wolf's head and hoped he'd understand it as reassurance while she gathered her thoughts.

"I will name you, if you decide that's something you want for its own sake," she said, knowing this opening was not ideal but needing the words out there anyway. Sure enough, the Wolf went rigid, and she rolled over in bed to wrap both her arms around him, their foreheads pressed together. "I don't need to name you to claim you, though," she told him in the secret warmth of her grandma's guest bedroom. "I can, and do, swear to take care of you. I swear to keep you close. And I swear that, no matter what happens—whether I name you or not—you will always be *my* Wolf."

A sudden breeze shook the house, a power raising goosebumps on Red's skin and making her squirm under the pressure. The Wolf gasped, eyes wide and shining in the dark, and he leapt on her like he wanted to burrow under her skin, wrapping every one of his shaking limbs around her.

"Thank you," he whispered, licking her shoulder and neck frantically. "Thank you, Red, thank you, yours, *yours,* your Wolf."

"Damn right," Red said, and she caught his mouth in a kiss.

The Wolf—much steadier on his feet now—walked her down the trail the next day, away from Red's grandma's house and Red's grandma's knowing smiles. He halted at the edge of the woods, looking beyond her to the farms, and further to the town. His tail lashed twice, and he gave her hand a squeeze.

"I will see you the next time you come to visit," he said, trying to sound relaxed about it and ending up somewhere in the vicinity of needy instead.

Red squinted at him thoughtfully for a moment. "Do you want to come with me?" she asked, not sure exactly what the issue was but willing to make a guess.

The Wolf's ears pricked up immediately, his tail wagging a little. "You told me to stay away from the farms," he said, instead of what he clearly actually meant, which was, "*Yes! Yes, please!*"

Red laughed incredulously. "You've been following that rule all this time?"

The Wolf frowned at her. "*You* told it to me."

Red shook her head, smothering a fond chuckle. "I just meant don't rustle the sheep." She tugged him toward her dirtbike, happy to see it was none the worse for having been parked on the edge of the forest overnight. "Come home with me?"

The Wolf's face went bright and joyous. "Yes, Red," he said, tail whipping through the air almost audibly. "I will."

"Hi, Mom," Red said as she shoved open the front door, and continued over the sound of Frankenstein's high-pitched yapping, "This is my boyfriend. He's a wolf. I'm pretty sure we're wolf-married, actually." To Frankenstein she added, "Sit! Shh!"

"It is an honor to meet you," the Wolf said awkwardly from just inside the door, three dogs and two cats all sniffing his ankles and Frankenstein sitting immediately in front of one paw, vibrating with his tiny Chihuahua (probably) desire to bark.

Red's mom blinked at her from the chair where she was folding laundry. "Well," she said after a moment of bewildered silence, "sounds like there's a story there."

Red glanced at the Wolf, a slow grin spreading across her face. "Yeah, you could say that," she said, aware that she looked goofy and lovestruck and just giving in. "Let me grab a snack and then we'll tell you all about it."

And they

(Red and the Wolf, at least. Red's grandma as well. Really, all the characters in this story, though we cannot make any assumptions about everyone in the world.)

lived

(At the farmhouse, until the Wolf finally admitted he had a hard time living around so many prey animals without being able to hunt them, and Red had a few conversations with her parents and her grandma, and they eventually moved into the second bedroom in the house in the clearing in the woods, which was better for the Wolf and good for Red's grandma to have an official witch's apprentice, and maybe, if she was honest, better for Red too.)

happily

(For the most part, because they worked at it.)

ever after.

Acknowledgements

I DID NOT PLAN TO WRITE this book. I planned to focus my creative energy on the next book in my Warrior's Guild series, with occasional breaks to write short fanfictions just for fun. As it has for many authors before me, fate and inspiration laughed in my face.

It started like this:

One normal morning as I was getting ready for work I cheerfully insulted Gyoza, our sixteen pound gray tabby cat, in the way many cat owners do. I cannot recall precisely what I said, but it was something along the lines of, "Absolutely not, you big ol' chonkus, do you think I can't see you and your giant paws trying to get on the cutting board?" probably followed by picking him up under the armpits so that he couldn't bite me and carrying him in front of the mirror to make him look at himself in shame. (This is not an effective method of cat discipline, but it's extremely funny.)

My brain then made a text notification sound and said, "What about a Red Riding Hood retelling where, when the Wolf is in Grandma's bed, Red talks to him like I talk to Gyoza?" immediately followed with, "What if he tries to bite her, but she trains horrible dogs so she knows all his tricks and escapes unscathed?"

Great idea, self, I thought, getting my keys and getting in the car.

An hour later I had written six hundred words on the clock at work, and two months after that I discovered I had accidentally written a novella.

Whoops?

This story would not be available in its finished form without the cheerleading and beta feedback of Nicole, who reads everything I write and leaves wonderful little gremlin comments in the margins. I would also like to thank Kenna Kettrick of Erudite Imp Editing for fixing all my typos, and for the several years of weekly workouts that we complain through the whole time. I would like to thank my cats, Matcha, CeeCee, and especially Gyoza for being the most unexpected source of inspiration for a story about a wolf. (I would also like to beg Gyoza to stop getting up onto the top of the fridge via the stove—eventually you are going to learn the hard way what a terrible idea that is, and I'm going to have to pay for your vet bills, you furry asshole.)

Finally, vitally, I want to thank my wife Crystal, who has very little to do with my actual writing but is endlessly supportive and never complains when I spend four hours on a Saturday frantically pouring words onto the page. I love you, babe! When you eventually read this, I hope you enjoy the furry porn!

Also by Scarlett Gale

The Warrior's Guild
His Secret Illuminations
His Sacred Incantations

Standalone
Red, the Wolf, and the Woods

Watch for more at www.scarlettgaleauthor.com.

About the Author

Scarlett Gale is the author of *His Secret Illuminations*. Long ago, under another name, she was the co-author of Needles and Artifice (Cooperative Press; 2012), featuring a rollicking romantic steampunk adventure novella and associated knitting patterns, of which she also designed several. She writes and produces fringe theatre plays based on B-movies, such as Bodacious Barbarian Babes vs. The Indigo Empress and Showgirls of Beast Island. She is a co-producer of the Alison-Bechdel-approved Bechdel Test Burlesque, which in 2017 was included in the Women and Gender Studies curriculum at the University of Oregon. She lives in Seattle with her wife where she gardens, knits, reads, and drinks warm beverages. Unsurprisingly, she also has cats.

Read more at www.scarlettgaleauthor.com.

About the Publisher

Unnatural Redhead Creations is the creative brainchild of the ever-versatile Seattle-based burlesque performer Scarlett O'Hairdye, encompassing illustration; graphic design; theatrical productions; costume design; and now: Romance novels!